UNDEF

He stood and listened to the darkness. It was whining and whispering. It was the night sound of the tunnels, the sound of Underworld. It was Stick's kingdom and lifeline, and his occasional hunting ground. If the girl was down there, Stick did not doubt that he could find her. He would hunt her down slowly and remorselessly, like a wolf running down its prey. He would track her like a beast and when he found her he would punish her. . . .

Scholastic Children's Books,
Scholastic Publications Ltd,
7–9 Pratt Street, London NW1 0AE, UK

Scholastic Inc.,
730 Broadway, New York, NY 10003, USA

Scholastic Canada Ltd,
123 Newkirk Road, Richmond Hill,
Ontario, Canada L4C 3G5

Ashton Scholastic Pty Ltd,
P O Box 579, Gosford, New South Wales,
Australia

Ashton Scholastic Ltd,
Private Bag 1, Penrose, Auckland,
New Zealand

First published by Scholastic Publications Limited, 1992

Copyright © Peter Beere, 1992

ISBN 0 590 55006 3

Printed by Cox and Wyman, Reading, Berks

UNDERWORLD

Peter Beere

THE FIRST TITLE IN THE
UNDERWORLD TRILOGY

Hippo Books
Scholastic Children's Books
London

Look out for:

UNDERWORLD II

UNDERWORLD III

Chapter One

The two runaways looked up as a shadow fell over them, momentarily eclipsing the morning sun.

"What are you doing?" the man asked.

"Nothing," Billy said. "We're sitting here."

"But you're sitting down in my piece of London."

The teenagers glanced at each other. They were in the middle of Trafalgar Square. How could it possibly be *this* guy's piece of London?

The man looked down on them, almost pityingly. "You see, I own this whole neighbourhood, and you have to pay for being in this spot."

"Pay for what?" whispered Billy.

"Pay for just being around here. Because I own it, see? I own the streets round here."

Billy and Sarah didn't know what he was talking about, but they were getting the message. The man was trying to lean on them, and looked quite capable of doing it. He looked capable of picking Billy up and throwing him clear over the fountains. He looked capable of flinging Sarah as far down as Westminster.

"But we're not doing anything," said Billy. "We're not harming anyone."

"That isn't the point, though." The tall man shook his head wistfully. He sat on the bench next to them and stretched his long legs out. His eyes were cold, and they never stopped watching them. "This isn't a free country," he said, "and it's a dangerous city, and you're new here and don't know what's going on. But you're going to have to be looked after, and you're going to have to be organised, otherwise, who knows what kind of trouble might fall on you?"

The man looked round the square, his grey eyes narrowing thoughtfully as he watched a flock of tourists poring over their patchwork maps. "There's all kinds of people on the streets," he murmured. "Bad guys and lunatics, gangs of troublemakers, people who want to

2

take away the things you've got. And so I have to look after you, it's up to me to take care of you. Because I own the streets, see? And you have to work for me."

Billy and Sarah had been in London for three days. They didn't know what to say to the man. They felt a sickening chill spreading through their veins.

"Otherwise," the man continued almost amiably, "your life will turn out a misery, and you wouldn't like that, you wouldn't want that at all. As for your girlfriend," the man leaned forward so that he could study Sarah carefully, "she could get herself into all kinds of trouble here. Young girls out on the streets – that's no fun at all these days. I'm telling you, you're better off working for me."

"We don't want your protection," said Billy.

"Oh, but I think you do, kid, otherwise you're not going to like it at all round here." The man gave Billy a smile, the way a cat might smile at a rat. "Yes you do, kid. And my name is Stick, by the way."

Stick gave them another cold smile, as Billy felt his heart sink slowly through his chest. This was not the way things were supposed to be at all. . . .

3

It had all seemed so easy a few days before, when they were making plans to run away from home. They were two ordinary teenagers living in Milton Keynes, with ordinary families, ordinary interests, going to ordinary schools. The only thing that set them apart was the fact that they'd fallen in love with each other, and that posed a few problems, when they came to explain the fact.

Their parents just couldn't seem to get it through their heads that Billy and Sarah were serious when they talked about the way they felt. When they finally *did* get it through their heads, they tried to come between the pair. It would have been easier if Billy and Sarah had kept their mouths shut.

Sarah's father, in particular, an accountant with the Civil Service, almost blew a gasket when he heard what they were talking about. They were talking about getting engaged one day, maybe they might even get married one day – but they were fourteen years old, and he blew his top. He threatened to sue Billy, murder him, take him to a vet's and castrate him. They had only just begun talking about it, they were talking about years ahead, but they couldn't get through to Sarah's father.

"*If you lay a finger on her, I'll kill you!*" seemed to be about all he could come out with. For an accountant, Sarah's father was pretty hysterical.

All of a sudden, Billy and Sarah were made to feel very young. And they hadn't felt that way before – it was only when their parents started treating them like children, instead of the adults they were rapidly becoming. Billy and Sarah knew what emotions were, they could feel them, they were living them – they didn't want to be sent to their rooms like two little kids who'd said a swear word.

It was getting totally out of hand – there was even talk of sending them to separate schools, and right before their eyes, their parents had turned into aliens. And though the teenagers' friends backed them up, they didn't have much advice to offer. They were all having problems growing up, it seemed.

It was the biggest thing in Billy and Sarah's lives, and the first time either had been in love. They shouldn't have been treated like children. Their parents had made a big mistake. It made them more resolute and convinced; it made them *want* to prove their parents wrong, and if they couldn't do it through their words, they would prove it by actions. They had tried to be reasonable, and had tried to explain, rationally, how they felt. In the end, they could see no alternative.

They talked it over with their friends, who weren't too convinced but could understand. In the end, Billy and Sarah ran away so that they could stay together.

The only thing they didn't count on was running into a hoodlum like the cold-eyed Stick Malloy. But it seemed whatever you did, there always had to be problems. . . .

Chapter Two

Against their will, not knowing how to resist
him, Billy and Sarah were brought under Stick's
influence. They were not the only ones; the pair
found out very quickly that almost everyone
around there was working for the thug. With
the help of his bodyguards, Stick controlled the
whole neighbourhood. Everyone shelled out for
'protection'; to protect themselves from Stick.

Billy and Sarah had a doorway on The Strand,
barely big enough to keep out the wind at
night. When they settled down in their sleeping bags they could listen to the other drifters,
to the dozens of street-people who had to jump
when Stick gave commands. They took what
sleep they could in the afternoons, and talked
their way through each lonely night, begging to
survive, to buy food, to pay off Stick's demands.

But no one ever complained, or if they did, they kept it fairly quiet. They didn't do it while Stick was around because he didn't like to hear arguments. He had a violent reputation and a temper like a Rottweiler. No one said very much at all when Stick was hanging round.

It wasn't the life the teenagers had hoped for when they were making their plans to run away from home.

This grim kind of life went on for a couple of weeks, until on the fifteenth day, something dramatic happened. It was getting late and Billy and Sarah were settling down for the night, trying to adjust an old umbrella which they'd propped up to keep the draughts at bay.

Tom, an old dosser, was bedding down in the next doorway, filling in the *Evening Standard* crossword with the remains of a broken ball-point pen. On the other side was Mary, an ancient woman who had walked the streets for years, with a bigger collection of bags and suit-cases than a coach-load of affluent holidaymakers. She always kept her doorway immaculate and scrubbed it out every evening. When she got her head down, her snores were louder than a passing Jumbo jet.

If Billy and Sarah had bothered to look out a little further, they could have seen that right along The Strand every doorway had its own huddled occupant. Groups of youths loitered under streetlamps, trying to keep their chilled spirits up. Video arcades stayed open all night, to take away what little cash they had. The first of London's revellers were heading for their homes, and people in hotels were thinking of settling down for the night.

Suddenly a scream lanced out of the darkness, and a scuffle started further down The Strand. Sarah poked her head out of the doorway to take a look. "There's a fight," she said.

Billy shuffled forward, dragging his sleeping bag along with him. He peered over her shoulder.

"Over there," said Sarah, pointing.

In the brightly lit driveway of a hotel, a group of men was shouting furiously. Something of a brawl had broken out, and two of the men were battling like demented apes; one of them had his hands round the other's throat, and was pushing him to the ground. There was a blur of movement, and another scream, then the sudden wail of a police siren. As a squad car screeched round a corner into view, the group broke up and ran.

They sprinted off through the night, and one of them headed Billy and Sarah's way. It was Stick Malloy.

He was running like the wind, his face tense as he threw a nervous look behind. It was a big mistake, because just as he passed them he ran straight into a middle-aged woman. They both went sprawling on the ground and the contents of Stick's pockets flew out and went bouncing and skittering to the edge of the pavement. Some rolled in the gutter, but he didn't have time to pick anything up; the police car was howling like a banshee in pursuit of him.

With an angry snarl Stick took off again, ignoring the prone woman, and vanished in the maze of side-streets which branch off The Strand. After a moment the woman got to her feet and walked away muttering and limping. The sound of the police siren faded slowly away into the London night.

Billy and Sarah didn't say a word for a while. They were both a little startled, and it had happened so fast that there wasn't time to work the details out. But they'd seen the stuff fall out of Stick's pockets, and curiosity was getting the better of them. After a little time, Sarah crept out of the doorway, and went to take a look.

"What is it?" asked Billy, as Sarah crept back with the things she'd found.

"All kinds of stuff," she said. "There's a knife – there's a man's wallet." She put the items on the ground and spread them out with her fingertips. "There's a little notebook. It's got Stick's initials on it."

Billy was staring at the wallet. "Wow, there's hundreds of pounds!" he said, as he looked through the contents, disturbing a thick wad of notes. "Look at this – this bloke's loaded."

"And look at this," said Sarah, quietly. There was blood on her fingers. It had transferred itself from the gleaming knife.

"What are we going to do?" whispered Billy. "He's going to kill us if we hand it back."

"And he'll kill us if we keep it."

The youngsters glanced around nervously.

Chapter Three

Half an hour later, while Sarah was sitting in the doorway on her own, Stick came back.

Sarah was wrapped in her sleeping bag, with her knees pressed against her chest. She was waiting for Billy, who had gone to buy some badly needed food. The pair had had no food at all that day and were positively starving; Billy had convinced her they could borrow something from the wallet. They would post the rest of the money back to its owner, and send the borrowed fiver when they could. They didn't think the man who'd been robbed would object, in the circumstances.

So Billy had gone to buy something, while Sarah tried hard to keep the cold at bay. But before he had time to get back again, Stick appeared, towering over Sarah.

She glanced at him nervously as he stood smiling down at her, his thin frame lit up by the garish lights of The Strand behind. He didn't seem to be in any great hurry, as he ran a hand through his greasy hair. There was something deadly and cold gleaming in his eyes.

"You've got something of mine," he said quietly.

Sarah felt a chill swirl inside her stomach. Almost instinctively she clutched the sleeping bag more tightly round her throat. "What do you mean?" she asked, feigning ignorance, though she knew it was a doomed attempt.

Stick gave a sigh. "Don't start trying to play games with me." He gave a glance down The Strand, towards the column in Trafalgar Square. He was checking to make sure there were no police about. "I saw you pick it up," he said, calmly. "I'm not stupid. Where's your boyfriend gone? He's gone off to spend a pile of my dough, has he?"

Sarah was shaking as she muttered, "I don't know what you're talking about."

"Don't give me that," he said, suddenly leaning down into the doorway. His body cut all the light out, so that she was bathed in his deep shadow. "I'm not playing games, kid. I want

13

the knife, I want the notebook, and I want the wallet back."

"Which notebook?" she whispered.

"The one you picked out of the gutter." Now that he was safe in the doorway, he was practically snarling at her. If he'd leaned any further forward, he would have landed on top of her. She could smell his foetid breath as it gusted right into her face.

Sarah hesitated for a moment. Then, "I haven't got it!" she cried, as the terror inside her became too much to bear. She tried to leap to her feet, and there was a sickening thud as her head smashed against Stick's jaw. He staggered back in surprise, clutching at his face.

"You little swine!" he said viciously, as he made a clumsy slash at her, but Sarah had wriggled out of the sleeping bag and shot beneath his arm. She could see that Stick wasn't fooling – he really meant to punch her in the face. He gave another furious snarl as she took off down The Strand.

She was running for her life, and people turned to watch as the two shapes hurtled by, for Stick was ten metres behind, closing on her all the time. They crossed the street at an angle, flashing between the swerving cars. Stick was yelling with fury as Sarah tried not to weep with fear. He was almost on top of her, his hand was reaching out to drag her back, when she made a sudden wild lunge, straight in front of a bus.

The driver slammed on the brakes as she bounced off the metal side. Stick made a grab at Sarah's sleeve, and tried to haul her back.

But she ripped her arm free, kicked him hard, and sprinted off again, seeing nothing in front of her but a strange kaleidoscope of bright and swirling lights. She could hear only the sound of her own breathing, and Stick's heavy footsteps pounding right behind. She thought she heard someone call out her name, but couldn't take the time to turn around and look. . . .

"Sarah!" cried Billy, as he dropped a Mac-Donald's bag and started off in pursuit, hurtling down the street.

But they were too far ahead — he was never going to catch up with them. He started calling out to passers-by, trying to get someone to help.

"He's going to kill her!" he yelled. Some people looked around, but they didn't try to help, for at night in the city no one wants to get too involved. They simply watched him tear past, and stared at the disappearing girl.

Billy ran like a madman, trying to cut down their hopeless lead, and as he ran he cried out, "Give him the knife, Sarah! Give him the knife!"

But Sarah couldn't hear for the traffic, and was too scared at that moment to try to work things out. Her eyes were blurring as the wind whipped frightened tears out of them. There was a terrible burning feeling in her chest.

Then the pair vanished in front of Billy, disappearing into the Tube station. He pounded in after them, in time to hear their footsteps fade away. Sarah and Stick had vaulted the ticket machines, and were heading at full pelt for the escalators. A station guard was yelling after them. Billy shoved him aside and was about to leap the barriers too when a hand suddenly grabbed him and dragged him back. "What the hell are you doing?" cried a voice.

"I have to go after them!" Billy tried to pull himself free, but the man had a firm grip on his shoulder.

"You can't go through there without a ticket," said the man, in a voice which didn't want to argue. He had had a long day, and could do without trouble now.

Billy searched through his pockets. "I haven't got time for a ticket. I've only got notes – and about ten pence in change," he said.

"You can get change at the ticket office."

"I haven't got time for the ticket office!"

"Well, you're not going through there," said the man patiently. "Go on, clear out!"

"But I have to go after them."

"The station's closing down. Where were you heading for?"

"I only want to go down there!" cried Billy, gesturing towards the escalators.

The man shook his head. "We've got enough trouble with kids round here. You're not going charging all over the place – I'll have the police round if you don't get lost. Go on, clear out of here! You young kids, you're just a pain in the neck."

Billy stared at him helplessly. "But he's going to kill her," he said.

"Oh yeah, sure." The man's face almost sneered. He had heard it all before. In his years on the Underground, he'd heard everything; there wasn't an excuse in the book he hadn't met. "Clear off, kid, we're going to close up the station soon." He shoved Billy towards the exit, and waited until he'd walked away. "Flaming kids!" he said. He shook his weary head grumpily.

The last train had just pulled out, and was clanking and squealing along the track.

Sarah stood at one end of the platform as Stick slowly advanced towards her, taking his time now, for there was nowhere left for the young girl to go. There was no one to bother them, there was nobody hanging round. There was just the platform, and the solitude, and the trembling, frightened girl.

Slowly he took off his belt and wrapped it tightly around his knuckled fist.

Then Sarah looked down at the tracks, and made a desperate leap. . . .

Chapter Four

Billy waited outside in the street for an hour, but they never came out, and the station began to close down for the night. The staff slowly drifted away, and the lights went out one by one. A dark and ominous silence settled over the place.

Suddenly Billy felt cold. He jammed his hands in his trouser pockets and paced up and down, but the walking didn't help. It wasn't the night that made him cold, but the deadly fear spreading through his heart. He didn't know where Sarah had gone. He didn't know where to begin to look.

A door at the side of the station opened quietly, and a man slipped out with a brown canvas bag under his arm. Billy walked up to him, nervously. "Excuse me—" he murmured.

The man stopped. "Yeah, what do you want?" he said.

"There were two people went in there, just before it closed. There was a tall bloke, and a girl in an anorak. They didn't have any tickets, and there was a bit of commotion—"

"Yes, I saw them," said the man. "Stupid buggers."

"Did they get on a train?"

"No, they missed it. It was already pulling out. It was the last one."

"But they never came out again."

"Well, they must have come out because they're not in there now, I've just checked the place and there's no one."

"Then they must have got on the train!" Billy blurted the words out. His eyes darted round desperately, searching the London night.

"I just told you, they missed it. I saw them myself, lad."

"Then—"

"Look, son, do you mind? I have to go home now." The man locked the door behind him. "I told you, they're not in there. You must have missed them. They'll be somewhere waiting for you."

"I've been here all the time," said Billy.

20

"Well, there's nothing I can do about it. It's getting late, son. It's about time you went home yourself. You can look for them tomorrow. They've probably gone home already—" The man was starting to move away.

"You don't think—"

"No, I don't," said the man. "I don't think anything. You must have missed them, so clear off and go back home."

Billy wandered the streets feeling totally desolate; he was scared, he was cold, and he was alone. He didn't know where to go, he didn't know who to ask for help. He ended up back on The Strand, because there was nowhere else.

Huddled down in his sleeping bag, all he could think of was that Sarah was alone somewhere, inside the tunnel system. On the run, in the land they called *Underworld*.

After a while he crept out of his doorway and walked to the next one. The old man had settled down for the night and was beginning to snore, buried inside a mass of fresh cardboard, with an old scarf wrapped around his face. Billy touched him. The old man nearly had a heart attack.

"Tom?" whispered Billy.

21

"What the heck?" The old man thrashed around. "What are you trying to do to me? Christ, I'm trying to get myself some sleep here!"

"It's my girlfriend—" Billy crouched down, and tried to lean into the doorway, to get out of the wind which was picking up. "You know, we're in the next doorway—"

"Yeah, I've seen you, so what?" said Tom.

"Well she's gone missing, and I think she's gone in the Underground. That guy Stick – he was after her, he chased her into the station—"

"She's gone into Underworld?" Tom let a low whistle escape from his teeth. "I'd forget all about her then, because she won't be coming back."

"You lived in the tunnels—"

"A long time ago, but I don't any more. I'm not like Stick – he really knows the tunnels. That bloke practically lives down there."

"Can you tell me where I'd go to get into them?"

Tom shook his head with resignation. "No, I can't, because you don't want to go down there. It's not natural – you should steer clear of Underworld. What we've got up here, this is luxury." He waved his hand at the brightly lit street. "And what's down there — well, you don't want to get involved. People go into that place and they never come out again. People get *killed* there. It's dangerous. You stay out of it."

"But you did it," said Billy.

Tom's eyes almost glazed over with despair. "And so do lots of people, but that doesn't mean it's easy. To find someone down there — it could take you the rest of your life. Have you got any idea what it's like? The place can drive you mad, dodging trains — they've got rats down there, they've got dogs, they've got gas, they've got poisons. That's before you even start thinking about the *people* who live in Underworld."

"But Sarah's down there," said Billy.

"Then Sarah must be out of her mind. She would've been better facing Stick up here than running round on the loose down there."

"Do you think she'll ever come out again?"

Tom grunted. "The question is, kid — is she going to come out again alive or dead? I mean, she might well come out plastered over the front of a Tube train. I'd forget it, kid. Go back home. It isn't safe round here. The streets are tough and getting tougher, but I'll tell you one thing for nothing — down there makes this up here seem like Easy Street." Tom settled down in his boxes again. "Like I say, I'd forget it, kid. If I were you, I'd go and find myself a new girlfriend."

But Billy couldn't forget about it, because he was lost without Sarah.

And they were in love. How could Billy forget a thing like that?

Chapter Five

Stick was angry. He couldn't figure out how he'd missed Sarah, but guessed he must have run straight past her in the dark. He'd come down a straight stretch of track between Charing Cross and Leicester Square, and there was no way she could have got there ahead of him. She wouldn't be able to outstrip him in the tunnels – Stick could fly like the wind down there. She must have found a hiding place, and he'd sprinted right past her.

This wasn't the kind of thing that would put Stick in a good mood, and his moods were fairly volatile and uncertain at the best of times. He stared back the way he'd come. She was probably hiding out back there. With any luck she'd have put her hand on the live rail by now. That way at least he'd be rid of her, although it wouldn't resolve what appeared to be his main problem: that they might still find his knife and his notebook on her mashed body.

Stick couldn't take a chance on that – he knew the police had their sights set on him. One way or another, he had to find the girl before someone else did. He had to find her before she got rid of the notebook, and somebody else picked his knife up. You couldn't leave clues like that around the place; the knife had traces of his blood smeared across it, it had his own bloody fingerprints all over it. Worse than that, the little notebook had details of his extortions and schemes in it. It even had Stick's name emblazoned across the front. He knew he should have got rid of it years ago, but it was so hard to keep track of things. It looked as though he was having to pay for his carelessness.

He stood and listened to the darkness. It was whining and whispering. It was the night sound of the tunnels, the sound of Underworld. It was Stick's kingdom and lifeline, and his occasional hunting ground. If the girl was down there, Stick did not doubt that he could find her. He would hunt her slowly and remorselessly, like a wolf running down its prey. He would track her like a beast and, when he found her, he would punish her. . . .

"Hey, Fatso—"

"What is it?" The fat youth woke with a sudden start. "What's going on, Boss?"

"Where's everyone else got to?"

"Erm—" The fat youth looked around. "I don't know," he said. "What time you got?"

Stick said, "It's a quarter-to-four in the morning."

"In the morning?" The fat youth's eyes blinked up unhappily. "It's a quarter-to-four in the morning?"

"Yeah, so what?" muttered Stick. "You want to make some big deal out of it?"

"Erm, er, no, Boss." The fat youth sat up and pushed a mass of crumpled covers off his podgy legs. "I was, er – nothing, you know, I mean – *four in the morning—*"

Stick switched on a wall-lamp, and the fat youth squinted at the figure slouched in the doorway. "No one's ever around when I need them."

It was meant as a warning, and Stick didn't need to repeat it for the fat youth to pick up the message. "Yeah, I'll go and wake 'em up, Boss." He struggled to pull on his trousers.

"And tuck your gut in – it's falling all over the place."

"Yeah, right, Boss." The youth grew flustered, and stumbled as he found his feet. He ran a hand through his hair, and tried a feeble grin. "I'll go and wake 'em all up, Boss."

"Yeah, you do that." Stick stood aside as the fat youth ran out of the room, sweating. He moved over to the bed and flicked on another wall-lamp, then picked up a magazine and flicked idly through it.

He glanced at his watch. From time to time he gave a weary sigh. He watched the doorway. He grew impatient, and tossed the magazine aside.

As he was starting to grow annoyed, four young men stumbled into the room. They were still sleepy, they were crumpled and half-dressed. They murmured greetings, but Stick wasn't too concerned about pleasantries. He waited until they were settled, then began. "We've got a problem. Some girl off the street has run off with my notebook. She's also picked up the knife we used on the job last night. It's got my fingerprints all over it."

One of the younger men grunted. He was a thin, rather greasy youth, with a deathly pale face. "What's the problem?" he said. "It ain't like the Old Bill got them."

Stick simply glared for a long time, then said, "Are you totally brainless? It's got his blood on it, it's got my fingerprints, and it's probably got *my* blood. You ain't ever heard of this DNA testing, the genetic fingerprinting they're using to track people down? Not to mention the notebook, which has got all our details in it. If that bloke croaks, they're going to do us for murder. How is that guy, anyway?"

"He died," someone murmured.

Stick gave a long sigh. "There you go then — it's definite. We're up the creek. If those kids start flashing that dough around, two young kids living on the street, someone's going to spot them and it's going to lead them right back to us. You lot are all in it, too, you know. We're all in this together. We're going to be hauled up for manslaughter if those kids get found."

A second skinny youth grunted. "So what do they look like? There are thousands of kids running round all over the place. How do we know where to look for them?"

Stick hunched forward on the bed, his thin arms resting casually on his knees. His eyes were deadly and distracted. "They've gone down into Underworld. At least, *she's* in Underworld. I don't know where the lad's got to, but we're going to make sure she never comes out again. She's a tall girl with long hair, and can run like a jack-rabbit. She's got jeans on, and a red chunky anorak. They used to live in The Strand, next to that brainless old woman. You've probably seen them around—"

"Yeah, I've seen them," said Fatso.

"Oh, well that makes all the difference," said Stick. "If you know who we're looking for, what in hell are we worried about?" The other youths smirked at the sarcasm, while Fatso glanced down uncomfortably. Stick continued: "She's somewhere in the Leicester Square area. I want all the local stations watched while I go in there after her. And I want one of you along—"

Fatso blanched. "You don't want me?" he said. "I hate it in Underworld."

"I'm not surprised," said Stick, scornfully. "You're so fat, you'd probably block all the tunnels up. You can organise the stakeouts, and I'll go in with Nuts. And we ain't fooling round with them. I want to get that stuff back again."

The other youths nodded their agreement. They were terrified not to. Stick wasn't noted for tolerating dissension.

"They could put us away this time, and I'm not being banged up for anyone. So let's get going," said Stick. "Before the stations start opening."

"What do we do when we find them?"

"We bake them a birthday cake. What do you think we do? We don't pass the time of day with them."

Chapter Six

Billy took some more money from the wallet. He bought a map of the Underground and a torch. He stuffed some food in his pockets, and picked up a lump of wood; if he had to fight to save Sarah, he wanted to be able to defend himself. He was feeling scared. He didn't want to go through with it, but occasionally there are things that you just have to do. It's all part of growing up, and part of finding someone you love. There are times when people have to fight for the things they want.

He went back to talk to old Tom. The old man wasn't in his doorway, but Billy found him sitting on the steps of St Martin's church, at the corner of Trafalgar Square. The Square was heaving with people and traffic, but Tom didn't notice them – he was far too tied up in his own affairs. He was rolling a cigarette with one grimy hand, and with the other he was trying to complete *The Times* crossword.

Billy's shadow fell across it, and Tom grunted as he saw the boy. He made some space so that Billy could sit alongside him. He carried on with the crossword for a while, and then put it down wearily. He said, "What's an eight-letter word for 'disability'?"

"I don't know," said Billy.

"Neither do I," muttered Tom. "I think sometimes these people just make these things up." He folded the newspaper away and tucked it inside his overcoat, and spent some time watching the life milling in the Square. Occasionally he used his hand to keep the sun from his eyes.

"What you up to?" he murmured.

"I'm going into the tunnels."

Tom snorted. "Then you've got a *mental* disability," he said. "A smart kid like you should stay out on the streets – you've got no place to move in Underworld. The darkness can drive you mad. I should know," he said quietly. "I lived there for eighteen months. Never again, though – I'd never go down there again. You should stick to your doorway, that's the place you're safe."

Billy shifted on the step. He looked a little uncomfortable. It was always uncomfortable when people offered you a different view. He said, "There are some things I want to ask you—"

"Like the way to the looney bin? You don't need to ask me," said Tom. "It sounds like you're heading there already." He stared between shifting lines of cars, watching the small flocks of pigeons feed. He liked birds, and often fed them with his own few scraps. "You don't really want to go down there. I know what I'm talking about. You don't even know if she's still in there."

"If she'd come out again, she would have come back to The Strand."

"Maybe," grunted Tom, and he stared away. He was looking down Whitehall, towards the buildings of Westminster. "Maybe your girl-friend's gone off you."

"Thanks a lot," muttered Billy.

"I'm only kidding you," said Tom. "But I don't think you know what it's like down there."

"I've heard rumours," said Billy.

"Yeah, we've all heard the rumours. But the

rumours, they don't tell you half of it. There's a whole world going on down there. They've got cities, they've got gang barons, food systems, intercoms – they've got it all worked out. The powers that be try to deny it, but it's all under our feet, Billy. Under where we're sitting, there's a world going on right now."

"Why don't they clear them out?" said Billy.

"How?" said Tom. "They'd have to practically close the whole city down. Do you know how many tunnels we've got running under London? There are thousands of them, there are thousands of miles, Billy. There are subways and the Underground, water pipes, sewage pipes, river systems – this place is mined by a thousand holes. And they're all underground, and there are people down there living in them. Clear them out? It'd be urban warfare."

"So they just leave them alone?" said Billy.

Tom grunted and lit his cigarette. It was as thin as a matchstick and burned like a fuse between his fingers. "Not if they catch 'em. If they catch 'em they turf 'em out. All I'm saying is, it ain't easy to catch people. They're like rats in a warren, so they just leave 'em be. Unless they cause trouble, in which case they sometimes go after 'em. There are special underground teams that go in there to hunt 'em down. Them that survive, what haven't already got sorted out. 'Cause they get poisoned by gas or drowned in the sewers, or ride the trains and fall off, and get crushed to bits. Or they get bitten by rats and die from that Weils disease. Or get completely lost, and go stark raving mad. They might even starve themselves to death, or go and drink some bad water – there's a million ways, and every one of 'em's horrible. That isn't a place you should go for your holidays—"

"I've bought a map—" said Billy.

"Ach, you want to throw that away! That kind of thing's no use at all. You have to find your way around down there by instinct." Tom gave a great snort. "You don't know nothing at all, Billy. And I don't even want to talk to you about it." He stared away moodily, watching the pigeons strut around the Square. He wished Billy hadn't reminded him of Underworld.

Billy was quiet for a long time. He had been hoping for encouragement, he had hoped that the rumours were a lot worse than the reality. But it didn't sound like they were – it sounded like the rumours were accurate. It didn't make him want to change his plans, but it didn't cheer him up either.

"So you think this is no good?" he said, holding his Underground map in the air.

Tom glanced at it scornfully. "It ain't even worth the paper it's printed on."

A shower of rain started to fall, pattering around them, making tiny dark spots on the streets. Billy glanced up uneasily, as if it were some kind of omen. The sun seemed to have abandoned the city entirely. "What about Stick?" he said quietly.

"What about him?" said Tom. He glanced up himself. He took the newspaper out and held it above his head.

"Don't you want to tell me about him?"

Tom shrugged his broad shoulders, and huddled down in his grey coat. He shuffled back into the sheltering porch of the church.

"What d'you want to know?" he said, finally.

"Is he as bad as they say he is?"

"No, he's worse," said Tom, scowling at the brooding clouds. "There ain't no good at all in a man like Stick Malloy. He was born bad, and he grew up to get even worse. He's mental, you know – he's an absolute headcase. He ought to be in an asylum."

"Is he as tough as they say he is?"

"He's tougher than that, Billy. If that guy's after you, you might as well give up. He don't ever let go, he's like a dog with a bone. Do you know why they call him 'Stick'?"

"Because he's so thin?"

"'Cause he *sticks* people – sticks 'em with a knife, Billy. That guy's a regular lunatic. He used to live in the tunnels for a while, ran a few of the gangs down there, but now he's moved himself up to the normal world. But he still goes back down there, 'cause that's where all his contacts are. Worse than that, I think he actually likes the place. That ought to show you what he's like, because nobody likes it there. But Stick does. Underworld's practically made for him. He can come up when he wants, disappear like a puff of smoke, and the police never even get close to him."

"I saw him stab someone," said Billy.

Tom twisted to look at him. "Saw him stab someone?"

"Outside the Palace Hotel."

Tom grunted again, rather cautiously, his eyes darting round the Square. "If you did, kid, you'd better keep quiet about it. Stick's got his men everywhere — he's got a regular empire. You keep out his way, 'cause he's a bad guy. A genuine bad guy — he don't just pretend at it. That Stick's a tough nut. He's hard, Billy. Very hard."

"I'm not really scared of him."

"Then you're dafter than I thought you were. You just keep out of his way. They say he once knifed a copper, though they never proved anything, but it was him all right, and one day they'll go after him. And when they do that, there's going to be real kinds of trouble; they'll tear Underworld apart to make sure they get him out. Keep out of his way, Billy."

"He's there after Sarah."

"If he's down there, you'd better forget about her."

Tom didn't say any more. He huddled down in his grey coat. And Billy watched the rain drifting across his face.

Chapter Seven

Sarah had made a mistake. Of all the places she might have run to, she'd picked what was probably the most deadly, by running into Underworld. It was a place where violence might threaten you, darkness make you go out of your mind, and solitude crush you like a tonne of bricks. There were a lot of people living down there, but Sarah didn't want to be one of them. Sarah just wanted to take herself out again.

But she was too scared to move. She was too scared to make a sound. She could only crouch in the darkness and shake with fear. She knew she had to start moving, but couldn't find strength inside her. Darkness had crept up all around her like a gang of thugs.

At least she knew some of the rules – she'd listened to them often enough, from other drif-

ters, from beaten losers, from those with rocks
for brains. They all agreed on one thing – you
don't make a move inside Underworld until
you're sure you know where the next safe place
is. It might be only a crevice, a crack in the
tunnel's wall, but it could save your life one
day, so you made sure you knew where it was.
You needed somewhere to run to if someone
came after you.

But Sarah couldn't find a place – she couldn't
see anything at all. In the gloom it was hard to
spot anything. She was only a step away from a
track filled with deadly force, and 600 volts of
power waiting to obliterate her.

Sarah couldn't stop looking at it. She
couldn't stop listening to it. It seemed to be
singing to her like a mythical Siren.

She licked her dry lips. She'd been down
there for several hours, and for most of that time
she'd been unable to move. She'd run out of
Stick's reach and, more from luck than through
judgement, had found a dark side-shaft in
which to conceal herself. She'd seen Stick running past, heard his breath as it snorted out,
and then the empty silence as the tunnels closed
for their nightly break. Every night the maintenance crews went about their work. She'd seen

one of their battery-powered vehicles go trundling by.

But the crew hadn't spotted Sarah, and she hadn't called out to them because somewhere down there, she knew Stick was waiting. And her terror of Stick was worse than her fear of Underworld. She would rather wait in the darkness than risk him catching her.

But she couldn't wait there for ever – she would have to emerge again sooner or later, and she knew that when dawn poured over London, the system would come to life. The night people would return to their world hidden under the city's streets; coming back to a world whose existence people denied.

Underworld did exist, though. Hundreds lived down there, crawling through the subways, the Underground and the service shafts. There was an entire world under London, and Sarah was lost in it, in the most deadly yet the safest of all places. No one would bother you, no one would come down to chase you out. You could live there, but first you had to survive.

Sarah tried hard to steel herself, tried to make herself take a step, because she wasn't ready to face Underworld's challenges yet. The people who went down there were driven by desperation, and she would rather take her chances on the city streets. She thought that at fourteen, she hadn't slumped to that level yet.

She took a long, steady breath and forced one foot to move ahead of the other. Keeping her hands on the wall, she slowly inched forwards. It wasn't far to the main track, and then she could find her way out; she could walk to a station and clamber out in the morning crowds. If somebody stopped her, it was better than being lost in the tunnels. She would rather be caught by the police and sent home again.

She told herself to watch out for the live rail, which was the one on the outside, because if she touched that she would never get home again. There would be a blinding flash and paralysis, and her problems would be over. She wasn't prepared for that yet. She had her life to lead.

She saw the main track approaching by the faint glow of the signal lights. With a few more steps, she would be on her way out of there. It couldn't be very far to the next station down the line. In the heart of London, nowhere could be very far.

She only had to take things slowly, to be careful, to avoid the power —

Then out of the darkness, a train suddenly

thundered past. It was only centimetres away from her and its drag almost pulled her on to the tracks, its noise filling the tunnels with a deafening roar.

Sarah stumbled backwards and screamed, clinging on to the tunnel wall while the wind whipped her hair and tried to tug her on. It wanted to throw her to the train, send her under its flashing wheels. Her fingernails gouged the wall as she howled with fright.

Then just as suddenly it was gone, with a *whoomph* and a rush of air; and the tracks seemed to thrum like phone wires in a strong wind. The very air seemed to hum, as if it tried to compose itself, and while the wall rocked with echoes, the sound rolled on and on.

Sarah was shaking like a leaf. She crouched, and wrapped her arms around her face. She didn't want to go on – she wanted to be some-how plucked from this torment and taken home. But she knew she couldn't find her way home until she'd survived Underworld. She had to outrun the trains, or she would not survive.

Chapter Eight

Stick Malloy swung his legs through a ventilation panel in the wall, and dropped like a cat on to the empty track below. He crouched for a while listening, and with nothing moving down the line, whispered instructions to a second man, who dropped down beside him. The second man's real name was Michael, but he was known by his nickname of 'Nuts'. He had once stepped on the live rail, and had survived to talk about it. Nuts didn't think he was fortunate to have achieved this slight measure of notoriety; the experience had frightened the life out of him, and he had not entered the tunnels since.

They didn't say anything. Stick was listening to the darkness. It was said that he could hear voices whispering. He could hear people kilometres away, as if his senses were specially attuned to it. Stick was a natural to exist inside Underworld.

"There's a train on its way," he said.

Nuts couldn't detect anything. He strained at the darkness, but could only hear silence coming back to him. It wasn't a complete and total silence, because there is always some noise inside Underworld, but he could hear no hint of a train, no sound of rushing power.

Stick was looking around curiously, as if the whole place enchanted him. "It's coming from behind," he said. "In about forty seconds."

This was an uncanny ability, and it made Nuts uneasy. "How can you tell?" he said. "How do you know there's a train coming?"

"Because you can feel the rails trembling," said Stick. "And you can hear the air whispering." Even as he spoke, Nuts heard a crackling, like the hiss of static electricity. He felt his back muscles tighten and the hairs on his neck rise.

"I don't like this—" he murmured.

"Just stay close to me," said Stick, putting his hand on the tunnel wall, as if to test its strength. "There are no gaps along this stretch, so we'll have to lie down and chance it. Just keep your head down—"

"*We're not going to lie on the track?*" cried Nuts.

Stick's voice was calm. "No, we're going to lie alongside it. If you keep your head down, the train will pass right over you."

"Er – I don't fancy this much—" said Nuts, who would have turned round and legged it if he could. But there was nowhere to run. They were trapped in the narrow shaft.

"Just do like I tell you." Stick suddenly pushed him down to the ground. "It's coming *right now*," he said. "So don't move a muscle!"

Nuts didn't move a muscle, but he couldn't keep from howling as the lights of a train hurtled into view. It seemed the whole world was folding in on him, as he wrapped his arms tightly round his head. It felt as though the Devil himself was breathing down his neck.

Billy stood on a platform at Charing Cross Underground station, and wondered if he had the courage to go through with this enterprise. He was trying to find the nerve to advance into Underworld. It was a test of the love that he felt, and the desire to turn round and walk away was so strong it made his stomach hurt.

He wanted to turn back. He wanted to race back the way he'd come. The only thing that kept him standing there was the thought of what Stick might have planned for her. Because if Stick got to Sarah before Billy could find her—

It was something he didn't want to think about. He didn't even want to dream of it.

He took a nervous step back as a train thundered out of the tunnel, rocking and rattling as it powered along the track. After a moment people clambered aboard. They didn't have to worry about what was going on underneath, on the deadly tracks. They didn't have to think about the power which drove the train on its thunderous way. They didn't care about the risks in the tunnels' depths.

Billy was thinking about these things, though, as he went through the rules again, the rules which said *run fast, run straight, and don't stop to think*. If you had to take time to think, it would already be too late for you. You would have become one more sad, desperate sacrifice to the speeding trains.

They were only the rules, though. The reality was that Billy now had to leap off the platform and make a dash down the deadly track. He had to turn himself over to Underworld.

He didn't find it easy. Other boys had

survived it, but they weren't Billy. This time it was his turn, and he wasn't sure he had it in him. He had almost convinced himself that he wasn't brave enough.

He was still trying to find a way to talk himself out of it, when a hand touched his shoulder, and somebody asked him if he felt okay.

That was the trigger Billy needed. He was right on the brink. A simple touch was all that was needed to send him over the edge. He didn't stop to think about it, he didn't look around to see who was there – he simply leapt, and started running instinctively.

Before Billy knew where he was, he was fifty metres down the empty track, and though someone shouted after him, he was too far gone to care by then, charging straight at the darkness and leaving the lights of the station behind.

Sarah was somewhere up ahead of him, and it was his job to lead her out again. He hoped it wouldn't take him long, because he still wasn't brave enough.

Nuts wasn't feeling brave, either. Nuts was

absolutely terrified. He couldn't even make himself speak for a minute or two.

Stick wasn't too good at offering sympathy. All he could say was, "You'll probably get used to it."

But Nuts didn't think so. Nuts didn't think he could survive it twice.

"There's hundreds of people down here. Don't be such a wimp."

The comment made Nuts look around the place even more cautiously. "That's the worst part of all. What are they doing down here?"

"Some of them live here," said Stick. "And some are just passing through. Some people come to hide out here."

"Yeah, but hiding from what?" said Nuts. "What could be worse than this?"

"There are all kinds of things to run away from." Stick zipped up his jacket as a cold wind gusted through the tunnel. "But right now, we've got other things to worry about."

"No, we haven't," muttered Nuts. "Nothing's more worrying than this. We're never going to find her in this place."

"You'd be surprised," replied Stick. "It's a lot smaller than you think. And we've got people at every station, covering this whole central area. We're going to find her eventually."

"And what will we do when we find her?" said Nuts. "She's only a kid, Stick."

Stick shrugged his shoulders. "That depends on how smart she is." He began to move down the tunnel. "We'll head on towards Down Street. I've got friends there who'll help us look for her. It was closed down years ago—"

"Closed down?" said Nuts miserably.

"Yeah, there are stations all over the place that aren't ever used any more. And they say Down Street is haunted."

With his heart in his boots Nuts trailed unhappily after Stick. He wished he'd been given a job on the station patrol.

Billy looked around nervously. The tunnel was whispering. He didn't know if it was his imagination or something to do with acoustics, but he could hear people murmuring; he could hear something rustling. He wondered how many rats might be living down there. And he wondered how big they might grow to if they bred without predators and control; he'd read a horror book about rats, and didn't like it much.

51

The book had been about man-eating rats that came out of the Underground—

He wished his best mate had never recommended it.

He kept glancing over his shoulder. He was sure someone was following him. He was also convinced that someone was waiting ahead of him. He seemed to be constantly surrounded by scuffling and rustling. He wished someone had thought of putting rat traps in the Underground.

Chapter Nine

She made it as far as the station at Piccadilly Circus, and then drew back at the sight of the waiting crowd. The station was heaving, there were video cameras set up on the walls, and maybe there were British Transport Police around. It wouldn't be very easy to simply climb out on the platform. She didn't think that would go unnoticed.

She went back down the tunnel a little way, and found a door set into the wall. It led to a passageway which brought her out in the station. Sarah tried not to run as she joined a queue waiting at the escalators. It was a relief to find herself out of Underworld.

She was going to head back to The Strand, to find Billy and start over again. This time they would—

Sarah stopped. There was someone she recognised. He was standing by the ticket machines, watching the bustling crowds go by. He was one of Stick's collectors – one of his ugly-faced muscle-men. He was one of the men who would go around making sure that people paid their dues on time, making sure they paid a rent for their miserable doorways. And as soon as Sarah saw him she knew he was looking for her. And she didn't doubt he'd be able to recognise her.

Sarah hesitated. If she made a scene, maybe she could burst straight out past the guy. But if the big man got to her, he would march her straight round to Stick. Without a ticket, there would be a big commotion anyway. She wouldn't be able to slip out quietly and try to hide.

She didn't know what to do. She went down by the other escalator, sat on the platform and tried to form a plan. But she was getting so tired. . . . She hadn't slept for nearly two days. It was getting hard to think – it was getting hard to even keep her eyes open. She'd had nothing to eat and her stomach was groaning at her. She couldn't concentrate, there was a pain starting round her eyes.

Then, as if she was dreaming, she heard someone calling to her, in a faint voice which came out of the tunnel. She looked around in alarm, but no one else seemed to have noticed it. She stood up and walked cautiously to the platform's edge.

Leaning forward warily, Sarah peered into the tunnel's gloom. There was someone down there. There was somebody calling to her. . . .

"What was that?" muttered Stick.

"It sounded like somebody shouting."

"What were they saying?"

Nuts shrugged his shoulders. "I couldn't make it out."

Stick paused to light a cigarette. "You hear all kinds of things down here. When you get tired, you can imagine almost anything. It's usually the wind in the tunnels, or a distant train, but in the darkness it can sound like anything you want. I've known people go crazy and follow sounds for days. They think it's calling to them — they think somebody's after them." He squinted into the darkness. "And it just keeps leading you on," he mused. "Till a train gets you, or you put your foot on the live rail."

Nuts looked across at him, miserably. "Do we have to talk about this now?" he said.

"You have to know," said Stick. "In case we get separated."

The thought filled Nuts with alarm. "We're not going to get separated!" he said. "It's bad enough as it is. I'm not staying on my own." He looked around in a panic, at the thought of losing his mind down there. "You can't breathe down here, you can't see or do anything."

"It's claustrophobia," said Stick. "You'll probably get used to it."

"I don't want to get used to it. I want to get the hell out of here!" Nuts felt his skin start to crawl as the darkness closed in on him. He got short of breath, he could feel horror rise in him.

"Take it easy," said Stick, grabbing hold of his shoulder. "We've only been here a couple of hours, and you'll start to get used to it. Any more of that, and I'll thump you one."

"Thanks a lot," yammered Nuts. "I didn't ask to come down here."

"But you're here now," said Stick, "so learn to live with it." He didn't have time for sympathy. "Because if I go down, we all go down — remember that. Either we find this dumb girl or we go down together. Take your pick – it's either this place or Pentonville. This is better than the nick, I can tell you for nothing."

"At least we wouldn't get mowed down by trains there."

"No, but I'll mow you down," said Stick, as he flicked the butt of his cigarette away, and set off once more along the empty track.

"Why didn't you bring Fatso along instead?"

"Because I told you, he'd never fit. It would be like trying to stick a whale in a sardine can."

Sarah stopped running. The voice had suddenly vanished. But she had been led deep into the tunnels, and was lost again.

She couldn't remember climbing on to the tracks. She couldn't remember which way she'd come, or how long she'd been down here. She was so tired that all she wanted was to find a place to lie down and close her eyes. She wanted to sleep away this whole nightmare, and wake in her own warm bed. She was cold, she was hungry, and the tunnel seemed to roll on interminably. She had never felt so utterly lost and alone before.

There was no sign of a station, no sign of another human being, Sarah put her head in her hands and cried with despair.

But there was no one to comfort her, there was nothing but the endless darkness. Sarah didn't know what to do or how to get away. She was lost inside Underworld, with only her own wits to help her out.

And then something started to howl—

She jumped up in alarm. There was something in the darkness ahead of her, moving relentlessly towards her. It howled again, and the sound chilled Sarah's very bones.

As she turned to run, a hand grabbed hold of her ankle. . . .

Chapter Ten

It was all a mistake. It wasn't a nightmare. The thing which was howling so fiercely wasn't a wolf, nor a beast from Hell – just a dog which was lost, and called out in fear. It had found itself separated from its mistress and, in an attempt to get back to her, had shepherded Sarah straight into her arms.

"Hey, watch where you're going!" cried the girl. "You're trampling all over me!"

"I'm sorry," Sarah said. "I thought someone was after me."

"There will be in a minute, if you carry on like that," said the girl. "You kicked my dinner over! What are you doing running round like that?"

"I said I'm sorry," declared Sarah. "I thought something was after me."

The girl frowned. "So you keep saying. What was after you?"

"I don't know," Sarah muttered, as she stared back along the tunnel. "There was something howling—"

"That's my dog, you great, blind, stupid article!" The girl got to her feet, wiping a mess of pot noodles from her lap, and clicked her tongue in disgust and frustration. "You kicked my dinner all over the place. What's the matter with you, are you crazy, or what?"

"I was *scared*!" shouted Sarah. "For God's sake, I'm scared!"

"Yeah, well welcome to the club – we're all scared down here. We don't go charging about, though, screaming all over the place. It's 'cause you're new down here, isn't it? You're a newcomer."

"So what?" muttered Sarah. "I just want to get out again."

"If you run round like that, they'll take you out in a coffin." The girl continued brushing at her jeans, trying to wipe off the stains with a length of rag. "Which would be a lot safer for the rest of us, I can tell you that. It's a good job these noodles weren't hot – you could have put me in hospital. What are you trying to do to yourself, kill yourself? Touch the wire?"

"I said I'm sorry," said Sarah huffily. "I didn't know. I'm new here, I've got to work out these things."

"Well, don't get on your high horse," said the girl. "I was just trying to help you. The way you're going, you won't last five minutes."

Sarah took a deep breath. She was trying to calm down. She was a little put out by the girl's attitude. "It's because it's scary," she muttered. "It's dark and it's scary, and I'm not used to it, and I just got a bit frightened, okay?"

"You frightened the hell out of me," said the girl. "You were like a pack of Millwall supporters. You nearly trod on my face, you know – on my face!"

"I'm sorry," said Sarah again.

"Not as sorry as I'd have been. It might not look much to you, but it's the only face I've got, you know."

"I'm not going to say it again!" said Sarah.

"All right then, you're very sorry. Now sit down, will you? You're in the way of the light."

"I can't help being big," said Sarah.

"You're so touchy! I never said you were big, I just said sit down! What on earth is the matter with you? Blimey, you're one weird kid—" She glanced back as she noticed Sarah staring down the tracks.

"There's a dog coming after us—"

"It's not *a* dog, it's *my* dog. He's not going to bother you. Will you just try to keep control? You're starting to make me feel nervous, you're getting me twitchy—" The girl sighed. She gave up trying to clean her jeans.

Sarah tried to calm down. She tried to stop her heart thumping, but she felt so weak, she thought she might faint. "Are you sure he's okay?" she said.

"He's over ninety years old," said the girl, and the look that she offered was disgusted. "Of course I'm sure he's all right – he's hardly got any teeth in his mouth—"

"Oh my life!" muttered Sarah.

"He's big, though."

A dog that looked like a wolf had padded out from the tunnel's gloom. It was slavering and snarling, snorting at the air.

"Is that him?" muttered Sarah, who had never been big on dogs.

"Yeah, that's him. His name's Sam." The girl beckoned the dog.

"He looks like a killer."

"He's not a killer." The girl pulled the dog's

lips apart. "He hasn't got any teeth, look – he's chewed them right down to the gums. He couldn't harm a sick gerbil, unless he wanted to suck it to death. He's a total baby, except he's about ninety-five."

"Dogs don't live that long," said Sarah.

"Go on – start picking a fight with me!" The girl's eyes rolled. "I've never known anyone as bad as you. He's a hundred in human terms," she stated defiantly. "Is that okay? In his own terms, he's about fifteen."

Sarah began to subside a little. She sat down beside the girl. "I'm sorry," she said. "It's just that—"

"It's scary, huh?" The girl became more sympathetic, and almost tapped Sarah on the arm. "You'll get used to it. We all do eventually."

That wasn't what Sarah wanted to hear, and she looked away miserably. "I don't want to. I'm only here for a little while."

"Yeah, that's what we all say," said the new girl. "And I've been down here for months now. But don't worry – you'll start to get used to it."

The girl's name was Nikki, and she was a

Londoner, from the middle-class suburb of Chingford. Things hadn't worked out at home, and after problems with her parents, she'd decided to run away. Her trip hadn't lasted long, and she went back two days later, but when the situation didn't alter, she'd gone on the streets again.

That time, she stayed away a little longer, before drifting back to her parents' home. The third time she left, Nikki decided to stay away for good. She was sixteen years old, with two younger brothers and two sisters. She had been living on her own now for the last two years.

Nikki had just turned fourteen when she headed off into the city's heart, and began to live on the streets which surround Covent Garden. Covent Garden is a tourist trap, with fancy shops and tacky restaurants, but at night it's a haven for the lost and scared. They can feel safe in the crowds and there's plenty of food around. There are plenty of doorways for sleeping in.

Nikki was smart, and the street life was boring, so she hung out with other kids and looked around for fun. Some of the kids were into graffiti and used to spray it on the Underground; they'd rack a store for paint cans, and bomb the trains parked in sidings.

It was a hazardous business, with security guards on patrol. They had a few close shaves, and all learned how to run away a lot. One day Nikki ran directly into the District Line, and found that she liked it; it was secretive and she felt strangely at home in there. She liked the feeling of solitude and the sense of freedom the tunnels gave. You could travel all over London riding the backs of trains.

Life on the streets was getting harder. There were organised gangs around, picking on drifters, starting to 'herd' them, starting to push them around. They began to make up protection leagues and were on the lookout for kids to use, to turn them into sneak-thiefs and steamers, to make them prostitutes. It wasn't what Nikki came for – she came to stop being pushed around. She began to dream more and more about Underworld.

One day she picked up some leaflets from the Transport Museum, made some enquiries, and decided she could handle it. She took her old, quilted sleeping bag and disappeared from the streets above.

She had made her home in the system for the last eleven months.

"I'm not going home," said Nikki. "I had enough of it the last time. I'm a lot happier here, even though it gets lonely. I've got plans for what I'm going to do, I'm going to be a librarian—" she reached behind her and tugged out a rucksack.

"See all this?" she said. "I'm studying. I'm going to get a few GCSEs. I go down to the library and pick up the course material. I'm not going to waste my time down here, because I'm not staying here for ever. It's just, at the moment, it suits me. But when I go out, I'm not going out with nothing. I'm going to take my exams and be a librarian."

"Do you like books?" said Sarah.

"Oh yeah, I really love them, I'm going to write some of my own one day. I've been making notes for the first one – it's like a guide book for people on the streets. And it's also a kind of adventure story."

"How much have you done?"

"A hundred and ten pages. The only problem is, I have to write it by candlelight. It's not good for your eyes." Nikki shook her head worriedly. "And the light level's really appalling

66

down here. You get kind of used to it, but it's blinding when you go back up."

"Do you go up often?"

"Yeah, I go up a lot of nights. I go to have a look round and get something to eat. And usually I steal a few candles!"

"I thought—" Sarah paused, and stared at her hands. "I thought the tunnels were – well, full of crazy people."

Nikki nodded. "Yeah, we've got plenty of them around. There's all kinds of people here, it's no different to topside. Except down here, people are generally quieter. We don't rush around as much, and we keep out of each other's way, but there's all kinds of things. We've got shops, we've got everything. We've got doctors and animals and—" she shrugged. "I don't know, really. Everything you can think of is around down here. Some people never go up again, they spend their whole lives here. Nobody bothers you, you can just make your own life."

"What about the trains going past?"

"You kind of get used to that. Mind you, you'd get used to being hit on the head by bricks." Nikki started to laugh, and her eyes flashed in the lamplight. "What's your name, by the way?"

"Sarah Collins."

"I'm Nikki Deveraux. Someone was calling for 'Sarah', yelling his head off, as if he was trying to find someone."

"I heard him, too!" cried Sarah. "What did he sound like? Do you think it was Billy?"

Nikki shrugged. "I don't know. Who's this Billy?"

"He's my boyfriend," said Sarah excitedly. "He might have come down to look for me. Did you see him? Where was he?"

"I don't know — back down there somewhere." Nikki waved her hand in the general direction. "Sound carries a lot, he could have been almost anywhere. Hey — where you going?"

Sarah was already running off. "I'm going to see if it was Billy!" she cried.

"You can't go charging around down there!" Nikki climbed to her feet, and the dog wagged its tail hopefully. She watched Sarah disappear around a bend in the track. "She's going to get herself killed," she said, after a moment. "I think maybe we'd better go after her."

Chapter Eleven

Nikki finally managed to catch up with Sarah, and grabbed her arm to stop her. "You're not going to find him," she said, "running round like that. He could have been anywhere, I don't even remember which tunnel he was in."

Sarah was panting, and her eyes were bright as she looked round excitedly. "I'm sure it was him, though," she said. "I knew he'd come after me."

"This really is true love," said Nikki, as her cheeks puffed out from running. "But if you carry on like this, all he's going to find will be a plate of meat. You're standing right in the middle of the Piccadilly Line, and they don't stop to move obstacles out of the way. We'd better get out of here — there'll be a train coming along any minute now."

Sarah felt a certain desperation as she turned towards Nikki. "But I've got to find where he is!" she cried. "I need him. We have to get out of here."

"Yeah, I know," Nikki nodded. "But not on the front of an Underground train, which is where you're going to be if I don't steer you away from this." She glanced down as the dog began to sniff cautiously at the air. "I think there's one coming. Sam can sense them – he can taste the air."

Even as Nikki spoke, the two girls felt a slight rumbling underfoot, and the dog began growling unhappily. "We have to go *now*," Nikki said, as she took hold of Sarah's arm. "You can look for him later, when the trains have stopped for the night." She began to pull Sarah after her as she headed back down the track, and they cut through a wide ventilation shaft.

On the other side they sat watching as a train trundled by a few metres away, spitting out sparks, burning oil, creaking like a tank.

"You'd better come back with me," said Nikki. "We'll go to my den for a while. You can calm down before you go charging round again." She touched Sarah on the arm, and her expression was a worried one. "Are you feeling okay? You're not going to start crying, are you?"

Sarah shook her head. "No. It just seems so hopeless," she murmured.

Nikki tried to cheer her up. "You've got to know what you're doing down here. You've got to work these things out. You can't go chasing all over the place. But if he's down here, I'll help you to look for him."

Sarah gave a slight sniff. "But why?" she said. "Why should you help me?"

"I don't know," said Nikki. "I sometimes get a bit lonely here."

The two girls walked side by side as they headed towards Nikki's den. And the old dog walked on ahead, growling at the air.

Stick was starting to feel a little crazy. He was getting frustrated that they hadn't located Sarah yet. Although there was a whole warren of tunnels around he thought he should have tracked her down easily. He had a big problem: he thought the whole world should be run for him.

Nuts wasn't so confident, and recognised the problem – you could hide an entire army inside

Underworld. He thought it was likely to take a long time, but didn't want to say this to Stick just yet because Stick had another problem: he didn't take kindly to advice.

Stick's frustration was obsessive, and it was also a little crazy; when things went wrong he took it out on those around him. It was Nuts who came in for some stick from Stick.

"I thought you were supposed to be tough," muttered Stick. "And you've done nothing but moan. It's getting on my nerves. Why don't you do something constructive?"

It was an unfair criticism, but Nuts didn't argue. Nuts could sense the fury that was building up inside his companion.

"It isn't my fault," he murmured. "I just don't like being down here. The place is so big, she could be hiding out anywhere."

"Oh well, that's brilliant," snarled Stick. "I wonder why I never thought of that. Of course she could be anywhere – that's why we've got to keep looking for her. I know this place, though, and I can smell her. I know she's still around. And I'm not going to get hauled up for manslaughter because of some stupid kid."

"Maybe she's not down here," said Nuts. "Maybe she's already gone out again. It's been more than a day now – she might have already gone back on the streets."

This opinion didn't go down too well with Stick. He didn't like being undermined by the suggestion that he might not know everything after all. He glared savagely at Nuts. "I know she's still down here. I can sense it. I said, I can smell the girl."

Nuts responded with a shrug of his shoulders. He felt that things were starting to get out of hand. The years Stick had spent inside Underworld were taking a toll of him. The darkness seemed to have crept in and poisoned him.

"I'm not going to get beaten by some stupid young kid," said Stick.

Nuts didn't answer. It wouldn't do any good at all.

Nikki had a small camping stove on which she boiled up some soup, then lit some candles to provide them with a little light.

They were in a small, brick-lined chamber, like a cave in the tunnel wall. It was shielded from the main shaft by a canvas sheet. It had everything Nikki needed: items of furniture, posters on the walls. It was a safe, cosy world, concealed from prying eyes.

"Once you're in here, you're safe," said Nikki. "No one can see you from the outside. If I could get a bed down, it would have about everything."

Sarah thought she had enough stuff; there wasn't room to fit a bed in. There were two mattresses, some floral armchairs, and a wooden desk. "Where do you get all this stuff?" she asked.

"I bring it down when it's quiet. You can get all you need inside Underworld."

"I just want to get out again. I don't want to live down here."

"Where do you want to live?"

"In a nice flat or something."

Nikki laughed. "Don't we all?" she said. "A flat here in London? What are you going to do, rob a bank?"

"We can do it."

"Who, you and Billy?" Nikki smiled at her, as she vigorously stirred the soup with a wooden spoon. She looked away. "I hope you do, but I wouldn't bank on it." She seemed lost in thought for a few moments, then searched out two china mugs. "When I get my GCSEs, I'm going to look for a place of my own. Maybe I'll share it with someone, I don't really know yet. I won't stay here for ever, but I really quite like it now. I needed somewhere to myself. Do you ever get that way?"

Sarah nodded. "That's why we ran away in the first place. Sometimes it seems there's so much pressure on you."

"Yeah, I know what you mean." Nikki poured the soup out into the mugs. "Get this down you. I've run out of bread, I'm afraid." She sat on the mattress, cradling her thin hands around her mug. "So you're definitely in love then?"

Sarah nodded. "I think so."

Nikki thought about it for a while. "How can you tell?" she said, curiously. "I've always wondered about it, how do you know when you're in love? How do you know that it's really love?"

Sarah blew on her soup, and moved her bottom onto a foam rubber mat. "I asked my mother once, when I wasn't sure either. She said, when there's someone you like, who you'd rather be with than anyone else, and you'd give your life for them, then you've probably fallen in love."

"Is it like that with Billy?" asked Nikki.

"I like him more than anyone else. I'd rather be with him than anyone else that I've ever met."

Nikki pondered on the point, while the soup mug steamed between her fingers. "I've never known anyone like that," she said, thoughtfully.

"You will do eventually. We all fall in love one day."

"Yeah, I hope so," said Nikki. "I don't think I've ever loved anyone. I seem to have always been a nuisance, just one more kid hanging round the place."

"But your parents loved you."

Nikki snorted, and turned her face away. "Didn't yours?" she said, after a while. "But you're not back there living with them. Sometimes it's hard. It's really hard to be growing up."

Sarah didn't dispute the fact. It did seem hard, growing up. And it didn't seem to become any easier when you got there.

"Particularly when you've got Stick running after you," she said.

Nikki looked up rather keenly. "What do you know about Stick?" she asked.

"He's the one who's been after me."

Nikki whistled between her teeth. "You don't make things easy for yourself."

"It all seemed to go wrong," said Sarah.

"It hasn't just gone wrong," said Nikki. "That's a total catastrophe."

Chapter Twelve

Billy stopped shouting. He knew it wasn't going to produce any results, but had to try it out of sheer desperation. He had stood in a tunnel and tried calling Sarah's name, but got nothing in return except echoes. The shouting made him feel conspicuous and vulnerable, so he stopped after a time, and just listened.

Water was dripping around him. He hadn't expected this. He thought the tunnels would be dry, but in some places they were leaking like waterfalls. The shafts were lined with iron plates, and the water found ways to wriggle through, penetrating cracks, dripping out to lie on the stones. Somewhere a great pump was pounding, trying to suck all the water away. There were 400 pumps in the Underground.

It had a sound like a heartbeat, as if the shaft

was a living thing. It was at once creepy, yet familiar and comforting. If there had been total silence, Billy thought he might have gone crazy. He didn't think he could have taken the darkness and silence for long.

Yet it wasn't even dark. As Billy stared down the tunnel's length he could see flickers of light breaking up the gloom. He could make out the tunnel walls, he could see rails glistening in the distance like the tracks of snails. It was better than he thought, but he hadn't been down there for too long yet. And he hadn't yet had to face an oncoming train.

That was the main thing that was worrying him; the thought of a train bearing down on him, travelling at maybe fifty kilometres an hour. There didn't seem a way of avoiding it, the tunnel was so straight and sheer. He could see no place to hide, no spot to shield himself.

A train would be coming soon, he could hear one back at Charing Cross. It had just pulled in at the station, and the automatic doors had hissed. Sound could carry well in the Underground, although it was distorted and unbalancing. It sounded as though the train was already just behind his back.

He glanced over his shoulder and saw the

train's light probing out ahead, snaking faintly round a curve in the tunnel's course. It was maybe two hundred metres behind him, and wouldn't take long to catch him up. He panicked and started to run.

The train driver checked back along the platform, making sure that everyone had clambered on the train. He pressed a blue button on his console, which made the doors close with a weary hiss, and when a light went out on a control panel, he dropped the engine into gear.

The train accelerated quickly, its wheels groaning at the strain, and began to rock gently from side to side. The driver peered straight ahead, looking into the darkness. It was hard to see, it was a lot more difficult than many people think. He was being guided by lights, and they could sometimes be baffling. But in a few seconds, the train had got up to speed.

It began to rattle alarmingly, as if it was shaking itself to bits. Inside a few moments, it was doing forty kilometres an hour. It was an old tr~in and had been around, but seldom produced any problems. It wouldn't take long for it to reach the next stop down the line.

The driver chewed on a mint. He liked working on the Underground. At one time he had trained as an engineer. Now he operated trains all day, keeping the heart of the city alive. Without the Underground, London would grind to a halt.

And he had seen some strange things down there. He had seen shadows which looked a lot like dogs, he had seen movement like people darting off the tracks. But he believed these were merely illusions, and there was nobody living down there. Because whatever people said, he thought that Underworld was just a myth. He couldn't believe anyone would live in a place like that. They couldn't survive. The movements were nothing but shadows, drifting litter, light distortion, the effect of tired eyes.

He stared straight ahead, then stood up on tiptoe as he thought he saw something racing down the track. It looked like a boy running flat out, with a bag bouncing on his back. The driver was about to turn on the brakes, when the strange shape disappeared.

Whatever it had been, it wasn't there now — it was just a trick of the tunnel's gloom. Perhaps a mirage, or a phantom, or a feral cat. There were cats living down there, he knew that for certain. But he'd never seen a boy yet.

There was nothing there.

Billy lifted his face from the dirt and peered after the disappearing train, amazed that he was still there to talk about it, and not a broken corpse.

The train had passed centimetres above him, and a trailing lead had clipped him on the head. It hadn't killed him, it hadn't crushed him. He'd been lucky.

But he didn't feel lucky – he thought it was a warning of things to come. He thought it was just the first shot in Underworld's deadly war. He didn't know whether it was the speed of the train, or its noise, or his own panic, but he'd suddenly realised that he was on the point of throwing away his life. The trains could not be outrun. If he hadn't stumbled, he didn't know what he might have done.

It was the stumble that saved him, because he'd pitched into a drainage pit. Another few metres, and the train would have dragged him on after it. He wasn't the first one to have tried lying under a speeding train. But he was one of the few who'd survived to remember it.

He knew he'd been very lucky. As he stood and dusted down his jeans, he knew that somebody somewhere had smiled on him. But it wasn't the kind of luck he could rely on. He had to get himself off the track. He had to give some more thought to his desperate plan.

He had to find a safe hiding place and lie low until he'd worked things out. The only trouble was, he couldn't see a safe place calling him.

Chapter Thirteen

While Billy was looking for a place to rest up for a while, he was being discussed in an office of the CID. It was on the seventh floor of a building not far from The Strand. Billy could probably have seen it from the doorway he and Sarah shared.

He didn't know either of the men who were talking about him. They'd never seen him either, but they were concerned about what he had. They were concerned about Sarah, for the very same reason. They were concerned, because they knew about Stick Malloy. One of the men had been after Stick for almost three years now. It had become something of a private crusade for him.

His name was Jack Renton, and he was squinting against the light slanting through his

Chief Inspector's window. He was somewhere in his late twenties, a tough-looking, handsome man, who didn't look very much like a police sergeant. He looked like a rock singer or a hooligan, in his sweatshirt and faded jeans. He had a black leather jacket draped across his back.

He was wearing a groove in the carpet as he paced up and down the room. He was restless, and his movements were short and tense.

"This is the best chance we've got," he said, using his hands to supply emphasis. "Because we've got witnesses, and they picked up some evidence. There's a bloke in The Strand, and he saw the kids pick Stick's knife up. He practically dropped it on top of them. They might have got other stuff too – the guy said things flew out all over the place. It must have been something, to make Stick come back after them. He chased the girl through the station and into the Underground. The boy's gone after them, and I think they're all still in there."

"What do you want me to do about it?" said the Inspector. It wasn't the response Renton was hoping for. He had been expecting a little more encouragement.

He turned away from the window. "I want to

go down there after them. I want to find them, because I think we can finally put Stick away."

The Chief Inspector leaned back and stared at him. He'd been in the Force a great many years. He knew all about Jack Renton and his 'Stick crusade'.

"What are you trying to say?" he said unhelpfully, as he toyed with his fountain pen. "That I should flood the whole Underground system with police officers? Just because some old dosser says there are two kids on the loose down there? And you think a thug like Stick's going to waste his time chasing round after them?"

Renton was about to interrupt when the Chief Inspector held his hand up. He wasn't in a mood to be interrupted by a subordinate. "I know you've got a grudge against Stick," he said. "I know he wounded your brother—"

"He didn't wound him," said Renton, bitterly. "He almost crippled him. My brother's still in a wheelchair—"

"I know," said the Chief Inspector. "But we can't afford to have men hunting round the Underground on the off chance. We've been after him for years, we've got six dossiers built up on him now. We'll get him eventually—"

"But not yet," muttered Renton. He leaned over the desk and put his fists down to support himself. "He isn't a fool, just because he's a thug," he said. "Stick's a very smart operator, and knows what he's up to. We could be hunting him till we're both past retirement age. If we don't get him soon he's going to do something really big, and it's a little late then to say we could have picked him up earlier." His eyes were glittering like diamonds as his passion spilled out uncontrollably. "I say we should get the guy. It's 'protecting the public'."

The Chief Inspector began to clean out his pipe with the end of his fountain pen. He stopped occasionally, to blow the old, powdered ash out of it. "If he's gone in the tunnels," he murmured, "it's down to the Transport Police. It doesn't come under our jurisdiction."

"But they're not going to do anything," said Renton, "because he hasn't committed a crime down there — it's all up here on the streets, where it's our concern. They've got enough things to worry about."

"So have we," said the Chief Inspector.

Renton had to turn away, because he was losing his temper. He walked to the window, pulled a gap in the venetian blinds, and stared out angrily at the busy streets.

"He's got an empire out there," he said. "He runs every scheme round here, and we've never once come close to getting hold of him. Do you know what I think? I think we should be a little more positive." He let the blinds fall back into place, and wiped his hands of dust.

The Chief Inspector didn't say anything. He was staring at Renton's back. He knew this whole argument was a throwback to Renton's wounded brother.

"I really want to get him," murmured Renton. "I want to bring Stick to justice. And I think that this time we might really be close to it."

"On the word of an old man—"

"He seemed to know what he was talking about. And I checked the station – they saw the two kids that night." Renton turned away from the window. "I want to go and bring them back, sir."

"You don't even know if they're still *in* the Underground."

Renton looked at him steadily. "No one's seen Stick around for a couple of days. He's got men at the stations, they must be looking for *someone*, and I think they're looking for those two kids. If I can get to them before he does, we can find what Stick's looking for, and it must be important for him to put all this effort in."

The Chief Inspector put his hand up again to calm Jack Renton down. He put his pipe in his mouth and started to chew on it. He was built like a mountain and the pipe was almost lost in him. He said, "We don't have the manpower to handle this. It belongs to the Transport Police."

Renton moved towards him excitedly, determination showing in every line of his face. "I don't want a big deal, if you'll just give me the go-ahead. I can find him myself. I'll go in on my own."

The Chief Inspector shook his head solemnly. "It's a personal vendetta, Jack."

"It's not a vendetta, sir. I genuinely think we can catch this guy."

The Chief Inspector seemed to be thinking about it, as he stared at his cluttered desk. His teeth made clicking sounds as they chewed on the stem of his pipe. Finally he looked up. "No, I'm sorry, Jack, it can't be done."

Renton stared hard at him. "He might hurt those two kids, sir."

The Chief Inspector shrugged his broad shoulders. "We don't know that for certain.

You'll have to wait for things to run their course."

That wasn't enough to satisfy Renton. He turned back to the window and peered out at the city again. "I have a back-log of leave," he said. "I'd like to take some of it now. I'd like to start right away, if that's okay with you."

The Chief Inspector sighed. "You want a holiday so that you can chase around the Underground?"

"It's my holiday," said Renton quietly. "I can do what I want with it."

"Not if you're going to go down there. I am not going to authorise it."

"It's my entitlement," said Renton.

"And I'm still in charge round here. I'm not having the police force dragged in on your private crusades."

"There won't be any trouble, sir. I just want two weeks' holiday."

The Chief Inspector sighed again. He took a deep breath while he thought about it. He suspected that if he didn't give Renton leave, he would take the two weeks off anyway. It would be hard to stop him, it could present problems either way. In the end he gave in and said, "But steer clear of the Underground. This is a police force – we're not vigilantes."

"I understand that," said Renton. "There won't be any problems."

He left the office, to prepare to go into Underworld.

Chapter Fourteen

Jack Renton's girlfriend didn't want him to go into Underworld. She thought he was being ridiculous. She thought Renton was playing the hero, and should have handled Stick in the normal way. She thought he was foolhardy, headstrong and stupid.

He couldn't really argue with her, she had a good point. But he was going ahead with it anyway.

"You'll end up losing your job," she said angrily. "Not to mention the risk down there. There are a lot of people who never come out again."

"I know what I'm doing," he said, as he packed a few clothes into his rucksack. "I've been there before, and I'm going to be okay."

"You're stupid, do you know that?" she said.

"It's never stopped me before," he said.

She took a deep breath, and planted herself right in front of him. "Stick isn't the kind of man you can just play around with. He's crazy!"

"I'm not playing around," he said. As he fastened his rucksack he couldn't make himself look at her, because he knew she was angry and disappointed with him. "I'm going down to look for two teenagers, who have picked up some evidence they have no idea at all what to do with. I'm going into Underworld to help them out, and at the same time put Stick away, because he's a lunatic, and shouldn't be on the city streets."

His girlfriend didn't buy that one for a minute. She said, "It's nothing to do with that. You're going after him because you want some revenge. You want to put him away because of what happened to Steven."

His eyes flicked up to look at her. "Is there anything wrong with that?"

Paula sighed. "I don't know," she said. "It doesn't feel right somehow. I don't think that police work should be like this."

Renton took hold of her hand, and led her to a seat in the window, where they could look down on the streets around Paddington. They had lived in their flat for two years, and had just finished the decorating. There was still a faint smell of gloss paint and air-freshener.

He took a deep breath. "I know I've got a thing about Stick, but that doesn't mean I'm completely demented. I know what I'm doing. There are two young people lost inside Underworld and, even while we're sitting here, Stick is down there trying to hunt them down. And he's not planning to throw them a party. He's down there because he's mad at them, and if he gets to them, I don't know what he'll do. Part of my job is protecting the public. Putting Stick away is only a side effect."

Paula didn't look at him. She was staring out of the window. "I don't believe you. It's because you're obsessed," she said.

"It's got nothing to do with obsession."

"He's got a thing about you too, you know. This is mutual. Stick's been waiting for you to come."

Renton stood up and sighed. He joined her in watching a long line of cars grumble miserably by. "So what do you want me to do?" he said. "Give up because Stick doesn't like me?"

Paula looked up at him, her hair falling across her face. There was a faraway look in her dark, worried eyes. "He knows you're after him," she said. "Just like I knew that one day it would come to this. There had to be a showdown—"

Renton shook his head slowly. "You've got it wrong," he said quietly. "This isn't about me and him – it's about justice, and I'm going to see that it has its day. He's got away with things for too long, and one day he's really going to hurt someone. Stick isn't normal. He's a genuine bad guy."

"And you're still the good guy?" she said.

He grinned. "Somebody has to be."

"You drive me mad," she said, shaking her head hopelessly. "I don't know why I love you."

"Because I'm cute and endearing," he said. "I'm a sweetheart."

"You're a pain in the neck," she said.

"You don't really mean that."

"No, I don't," she said gravely. "The truth is, you're making me worry about you."

That made him pause for a moment, as he reached down to stroke her cheek. She didn't take his hand, but she leaned in against his touch.

"You don't have to be worried," he said. "I can take care of myself."

"No, you can't," she said. "You're still a big kid inside."

She watched him finish his packing, wishing with all her heart that he wouldn't go. But Renton had already made up his mind. She was never going to convince him, and the thought made her miserable. She prayed he'd come back to her again.

Chapter Fifteen

Nikki drained the last of the soup from her china mug. She cleaned the mug on a length of cloth, put it away on a shelf, then cleaned out the saucepan and shoved it into a cupboard. She did a quick bit of tidying up, but seemed a little tense about things. She kept glancing up, listening to the darkness.

"We shouldn't stay around here if Stick's in the neighbourhood. We ought to move on and find somewhere safer. Maybe we ought to head westward, to the other side of London, at least until he's given up looking for you. What do you think?" she said, looking round, brushing a thin strand of hair from her eyes. She peered through the soft, yellow candlelight at Sarah.

Sarah didn't answer. She had fallen asleep. She was slumped across the mattress with her knees sticking in the air. Sarah hadn't rested for two days and the strain had suddenly caught up with her. Her half-finished mug of soup was balanced precariously on her chest.

Nikki sat and watched her for a time, then eased the mug out of Sarah's fingers, and quietly put it on the floor at the side of the bed. She picked up a blanket and spread it gently across her, then eased Sarah's head onto a thick feather pillow. Sarah didn't respond to any of it. She was practically unconscious. She couldn't remember ever having been quite so weary.

Nikki sat back again, frowning uneasily at the shadows. She was getting worried; she knew all about Stick's vicious ways. She didn't want him bursting in on them in his search for his notebook. She didn't think they'd stand much chance trying to fight him off.

And she didn't feel safe there. It was too close to Charing Cross, too close to the area that Stick would be looking in. It was fairly clear they had to move on, but they could maybe delay it till the evening, at least until Sarah had had some rest.

She was thinking of going over to Hammersmith, where she had a few friends, and they could hide out until Stick had given up on them. It would entail a hazardous journey through the centre of Underworld, through the deep-lying tunnels of the Piccadilly Line. But it was better than waiting for Stick to catch up with them, and Stick was pretty determined. She knew that sooner or later, Stick would track them down.

Nikki was getting low on supplies, though, and they'd need to take something to keep their strength up. Carefully she checked through her food supplies. It wasn't much, just enough for a day or two. Things didn't look very promising — they could have done with a lot more than that. She decided to slip out for a short while, to buy extra stuff.

She sorted through her pockets and got all her money together, finding five pounds in change and a crumpled dollar bill. She'd found the bill in Covent Garden and kept it in case she ever went to America. At that moment, she would have settled for Hammersmith.

She glanced at Sarah again, and decided not to disturb her, picked up her bag and backed quietly out of the den. It would take the best part of an hour, then a couple of hours to get sorted out. They would be ready to move on to Hammersmith in the evening.

She put the canvas sheet back into place, and slipped away through the darkness, her old dog trotting happily at her heels.

At almost the same moment Jack Renton was cautiously lowering himself into the tunnels of Underworld. He had entered by a service shaft at Charing Cross station, which brought him out in a tunnel to the west of the platforms. The first thing he saw was a dead cat lying stiff at his feet. There was no one around, and the air was stale and dry.

He didn't know how to find Stick, other than to keep roaming around generally, in the hope of finding someone who had seen the man. He couldn't make too much fuss about it because he wasn't supposed to be down there, and the Police had never been too welcome in Underworld.

He felt uneasy – the place was filled with menace and mystery. He hoped it wouldn't take him too long to find the teenagers. The longer he stayed down there, the more risks he would have to run, and there were plenty of risks inside Underworld.

He listened to the noises drifting out of the

darkness. They seemed to be whispering secretly.

He glanced over his shoulder as he set off down the westbound track. The dead cat appeared to be watching him. But it did not say anything.

Half-way to the surface, Nikki felt a few doubts. She wasn't sure about leaving Sarah on her own. Sarah might get upset if she woke up and found herself abandoned, and she'd be on her own if Stick chanced to discover her. Nikki thought she should have stayed with her and kept Sarah company. She should have stayed there and tried to protect her friend.

She began to backtrack, and then paused. She would have to get someone to go for her, and trust them to bring food back. She decided to find a young vagabond called Johnny D. He usually hung out in a side-tunnel which he shared with some other lads. He was like a bloodhound – he could find just about anything. The only problem was that he could sometimes be difficult to track down. Johnny had the gift of being able to disappear like a will o' the wisp.

But Nikki was lucky; she found him sitting at the entrance to the side-tunnel, whittling away on a piece of wood. She wasn't sure what he was whittling but it looked like a small spear. She didn't like to think what he might be planning to use it for.

He glanced up as she approached, but his face didn't alter, so that it was hard to know what he was thinking about. He had the body of a youngster, but the face of an older man. He could have been twelve, or twenty-five, or maybe forty-two.

"Hello, Johnny," she said, as she crouched down beside him. "What are you whittling?"

"An assegai. I'm going rat-hunting." He spoke very softly, as if he had years of experience under his belt. But your first guess would have been right – he was only twelve years old.

He put the spear to one side and gave Nikki a sideways look. He had a sharp-featured, dark, rather handsome face. "What can I do for you?" he said, gravely.

"I wanted some shopping."

"What's wrong with your legs, then?" He glanced at them pointedly.

"Nothing," said Nikki, as she shifted on her heels. "I just don't feel like going out. Will you go and get me some?"

Johnny shrugged his thin shoulders. "Sure, okay," he said finally. "As long as I get something."

"I'll give you a pound," she said.

"*A pound?*" Johnny didn't seem too impressed with the offer.

Nikki shrugged. "I haven't got much, and I need to buy the stuff."

Johnny D. thought about it for a while. "Well, okay. What do you want?" he said.

Nikki gave him her shopping bag. It was a green plastic *Harrods* bag. She'd never bought anything there, but liked the bags they gave. "A loaf of bread, tins of baked beans, some biscuits and bananas, and two tins of dog food, as long as it's cheap stuff."

"You don't want to give me the dog?" murmured Johnny, turning round to take a look at Sam.

"What do you want him for?"

"I could sell him as a guard dog."

"He's too old for that," said Nikki, as she tipped her money into Johnny's palm. "Get what you can with it."

"Should I bring it to your place?"

Nikki nodded, and stood up. "Can you get it

pretty quickly?"

"What, right now?"

"Yeah, if you're not doing anything."

Johnny stared at her and shrugged. He looked a little disgruntled as he toyed with the money and counted it. "Okay," he said moodily, then watched as she disappeared into the tunnel system. He wondered why she was not going out herself. Maybe there was something going on that it might be useful to know about. People acting strangely could sometimes prove profitable.

He poked his head into the side-tunnel and said, "I'm going to be gone for a while."

It might be worth spending some time watching Nikki Deveraux.

Chapter Sixteen

There was usually a man walking around selling groceries off a handcart he pushed down the side of the track. But no one had seen him about for a while, and there was a rumour going around that he'd been hit by a train on the Northern line. This wasn't an uncommon occurrence, but proved a mite inconvenient, as it meant that Johnny had to go topside to get Nikki's food.

He went into a supermarket, where he didn't bother with the niceties but stuffed the things Nikki wanted straight inside his coat. That way he could slip out of a side door and keep her money, because he wouldn't get rich if he had to go through life paying for things. He was an Artful Dodger of the Underworld, and had designs to make it big one day.

He went back into the tunnels through a door

used by cleaners and electricians, still deep in thought about Nikki and what was going on. He had an instinctive sense for the main chance, and this particular lead appeared promising. Johnny had no conscience, but then, had never thought to ask for one.

He approached her den warily, keeping his eyes peeled, his ears cocked, and his senses on overtime. Nikki came out a long way to meet him, and that was also a little puzzling. She watched him cautiously. "I'll take it from here," she said.

He eyed her warily. "Okay," he said, and tried to take a sneaky look past her, but she moved almost casually to block his view. She took the bag from his hand and stood with it swinging from her fingertips.

"Did I get any change?" she asked.

He shook his head. "No, I spent it all."

Nikki snorted. She knew what he'd done, but couldn't make too much fuss about it. If she'd gone herself, she'd have spent the cash anyway. "Okay," she said. "Thanks."

"Yeah. I'll see you around," he said. Then he strolled away slowly, with his hands in his trouser pockets.

She stood and watched until he disappeared,

and then slipped back inside her den. Sarah woke up as the bag broke and cans rolled across the floor.

"What's going on?" she said.

"Nothing. Go back to sleep," Nikki murmured.

As Sarah turned over, Nikki packed the goods into a canvas bag.

She didn't trust Johnny D. too much, although she didn't know what he could do to her, but all the same she felt the need to check outside the den. She was starting to get jumpy with the thought that Stick was stalking around the place. She would be glad when the time came to move along.

Johnny hung around for a while but nobody came out of Nikki's den, and he decided he could be in for a long, lonely wait that night.

He took out a *Snickers* bar and chewed on it thoughtfully. All things come to those who wait.

"I don't believe it!" said Nuts.

"What's the matter with you now?" said Stick.

"I've just gone and trod in some dog muck."

"Well, watch where you're going then." Stick didn't have too much sympathy for Nuts. Stick had far too many other things on his mind.

They were getting close to Down Street station, situated between Green Park and Hyde Park Corner. It was a station which had been closed down in 1932 and was rumoured to be haunted, but that didn't stop a succession of people from setting up home in it. The people in there at the moment were a group of young drifters. They survived by stealing handbags from the regular train travellers.

The place itself had been panelled off from the main Piccadilly line, but a door had been carefully cut in the wood. It would have been hard to find if you knew it was there and were actively looking for it, but Stick could have walked to it blindfolded. It wasn't a problem to him, because he himself had put it there.

On the far side was an encampment which ran the entire length of the platform. It was like a small town. It took Nuts' startled breath away.

"Bloomin' 'eck!" he said quietly. "Where did all these guys spring from?"

"They live here," said Stick, pushing his way through the crowd.

Nuts trotted behind with his mouth hanging open, trying to make some kind of sense of the things he saw. But he couldn't manage it. He seemed to have been thrown into a different world.

The scene was near bedlam. There were two hundred people living there, in a collection of shelters and canvas tents. The air was smoky and pungent with an assortment of fragrances – the scent of oil lamps and foodstuffs, the stench of animals. They could see pigeons and dogs strutting around, and a goat which had lost its ears. They could see people dressed in rags, and some in finery. It was like a market in the Orient or a nomadic camp on some sandy plain. It was like a wildman's fantasy, or a drunken artist's mad, exotic dream.

For a moment Nuts was helpless, and couldn't voice what he felt inside. He wasn't sure if he was delighted, or amazed, or slightly horrified. "It's like the Ark," he said, gazing round. "It's like some place from the Dark Ages. They look like savages."

"No, they're just like you and me," said Stick.

He stepped over a bawling child and pushed his way through a beaded screen. A startled chicken flew towards him on a rush of wings.

A bearded man with scars on his face, like he'd tried to tattoo himself and mucked it up, looked up and waved a hand to try to clear the air. "Is that you?" he said.

Stick grinned. "Yeah, I said I'd be back again."

The scarred man grunted. "Yeah. We hoped you were just kidding us."

Chapter Seventeen

Nuts was silent, stunned by the squatter-camp which existed in the Underground system. He'd been around a lot and had seen many strange things, but nothing he had ever seen appeared quite so bizarre as that hotchpotch collection of vagabonds.

In many ways their life seemed ideal: there were no laws but their own laws, there was no one they had to answer to, but those they chose. And yet it was not idyllic – there were other problems.

They were having a big problem that day. They had come into conflict with another gang, and were suffering from the effects of a recent raid. A gang which worked around Islington had moved down to their area and ransacked the camp on the previous night. They had passed through like a tribe of banshees and torn the whole place apart; they had run off with livestock and foodstuff and precious goods. There had been a lot of violence in their passing, and a lot of misery in the aftermath. The only way the group knew to respond was to fight back. A raid could not go unanswered, and already retaliation was being prepared. The Down Street gang had little time left to spare for any problems Stick might have.

Stick was beginning to lose his cool. He had come to enlist sympathy and support for his cause, but instead found himself pushed to one side of a milling throng. And Stick didn't like being shoved aside – he wanted people to gather round and help him out. He wanted everyone to be as keen on finding the two teenagers as he was.

It took Stick a long time to realise that that wasn't going to happen, and that the group had enough problems of their own that day. They were still trying to recover to check through their casualties. It took him a while to appreciate that most of them had not even noticed him.

Stick had a certain kind of brooding insanity in his character, and it was beginning to rise to the surface as he found himself steered into a ticket hall, which had last seen a customer way back in 1932. What he wanted to do was grab hold of someone and scream at them. He wanted to say, *"Will you sit down and listen a minute!"*, but they were too busy rushing round, shouting and waving their hands in the air. What Stick really needed was patience, but he'd never even heard of it. He almost snarled when the leader finally sat down with him.

"How you doing, Stick?" said the man, without interest. He was forty years old, a great, bruising bear of a man, with his chest and arms covered in tattoos. He wore a pair of grey dungarees and had a scarf knotted round his neck. His beard was big enough to hide chickens in.

"What's going on round here, then?" said Stick, sullenly.

The man grunted. "A little trouble we had last night. Some crew came down out of Islington and tried to mess us up. We're going to go there tonight and let them have a taste of their own medicine. Want to come along?"

"No, I've got problems of my own," said Stick. He didn't look too ecstatic. He didn't even look happy. He was still nursing a temper from having found himself ignored for so long.

But the big man wasn't too bothered. He sat down and chewed on a matchstick. He looked as though he'd rather be watching coats of paint dry on a distant wall. "What brings you here?" he said finally.

Stick tried to look casual. He didn't want it to seem as though he actually needed something. "I was looking for someone," he murmured, examining the sole of his boot. "I thought some of you guys might want to help me take a look for her, what with us being such really close buddies and all, and me having helped you out enough times in the last few months."

"Who are you looking for?" said the big man.

"Just a girl. She's a runaway."

"What's she done?"

Stick's eyes glanced up and stared at him impassively. "That part of it's my affair."

The big man wasn't intimidated. He might have been a short time ago, when Stick was practically running Down Street station. But now Stick had moved on and he'd been left in charge of things. He had plenty of friends around to help him out. "What's her name?" he said finally.

"I don't know," said Stick moodily. "Susan, or something. Patricia. How the hell should I know?"

The big man grinned. "That's a lot of help." He looked over his shoulder as a group of children galloped past, screaming their heads off. "I don't think anyone's going to be falling all over themselves to go out looking for runaways."

Stick glared back at him with a deadly intensity. "It's a favour," he muttered. "I was asking for a favour." He was starting to hate the big bearded man.

"We've got enough problems of our own," said the man. "Didn't you see, coming in? The whole place looks like a bomb site. It's a mess down there."

Stick wasn't concerned about that. He wanted people to rush round to help him out, and he had Nuts sitting there, quietly watching him. "That's a big help," he muttered. "After all I've done for you. If it wasn't for me, you know, you wouldn't even be in this place."

The man stared back at him calmly. "But then, you're not so big any more. People aren't as afraid of you as they might have been once before."

"Oh yeah?" Stick sprang to his feet, and seemed to think better of it. He took a deep breath, then lowered himself back into the chair. He spread his hands in the air and tried to put on a friendly look. "All I'm asking you for is a favour. It isn't too much to ask."

The man continued to stare back at him. "We've got problems of our own," he said. "We don't need your problems. Why can't you find this girl on your own?"

"I can," muttered Stick. "I was just asking a favour." He didn't want to admit that he was having problems tracking Sarah down. "But if you don't want to help me—" he was trying to bluff his way out of the situation and he was in danger of losing face right in front of the watchful Nuts. "If you can't help a friend out—"

The man shrugged. He didn't give a monkey's, really. He wouldn't care if he never had to see Stick's white face again.

"Well, I'll be on my way then," said Stick. "I'll maybe see you around some time."

"Yeah. Maybe see you around," said the man.

Stick stood up and prepared to leave, and

found he'd been sitting in some bird-droppings. "But don't ever come round and ask *me* for a favour again."

The man gave him a faint smile. "I think we'll manage without you," he said.

Stick grunted. "Lots of luck," he said. "I hope you choke yourself." Then he walked away stiffly, with Nuts trotting at his heels. When they were out of earshot he said, "I really can't stand that guy."

Back at the station, the big man was talking to his companions. He stared after Stick. "You know, that guy is an absolute berk," he said.

"What are we going to do now?" enquired Nuts, as the two men went back into the tunnel system.

"How do I know?" growled Stick. "Just shut up, will you?"

He didn't feel much like talking about it, and didn't even want to have to start thinking about it. The whole business was a pain in the neck. He was getting sick of these problems, and wanted to kick someone's brains in. But he only had Nuts there, and didn't think that he had any.

So he strode on in a sulk, as Nuts trotted miserably after him.

Nuts thought it was Stick who had problems in the brain department.

Chapter Eighteen

Johnny glanced up as a youth came towards him. His clothes were soiled and crumpled, his hair like a ragged mop and his eyes like dark pits in his pallid face. From the way the boy's face was twisted up he might have been suffering from stomach ache, but it was just an expression of his misery.

"Hi," he said wearily, as he stopped in front of Johnny, and crouched on his heels like a sick old man. "There's a lot of walking round here," he sighed. "I've been walking all over the place."

"What do you expect?" muttered Johnny. "This is Underworld." He shifted his position slightly, so that the guy wouldn't trample all over him. "You won't find a bus stop, if that's what you're looking for."

The boy nodded. "I suppose not," he said. "I guess you're right." He watched the ground dismally, looking tired and dispirited. His blue eyes were bloodshot, and his lips seemed dry. "My name's Billy."

So what? thought Johnny.

"I'm looking for someone. I'm looking for my girlfriend. Have you seen her?"

Johnny shrugged, and didn't bother to say anything. He was unlikely to help unless it looked as though there was something in it for him. He wasn't in the business of playing Samaritans. "What does she look like?"

"She's er, tall, about my height, with long hair and brown eyes. She's wearing an anorak. Her name's Sarah."

Johnny looked away. "No, I don't think I've seen her."

"Oh." Billy's face fell, and he looked down dejectedly. He stared at the ground again. "I've been looking all over for her. I haven't slept."

What a berk, Johnny thought to himself.

"She came down two days ago. I don't even know if she's still down here." Billy felt a great need to discuss all his problems. He wanted to share them with someone, even an absolute stranger, even with a young kid who looked like some kind of weasel. "I don't even know where to start looking." He let his shoulders shrug hopelessly. "I can't sleep, I can't settle anywhere. I don't know anyone."

Johnny didn't offer any comfort, or give a word of encouragement. He didn't do a thing but look bored, and sigh noisily.

"I guess it's a big place," said Billy, his gaze still fixed on the oil-stained ground.

"Well, it would be," said Johnny. "It's London, isn't it?"

Billy nodded, and stood up. He could see he wasn't going to get anywhere. It seemed that in Underworld you had to sort out these things yourself. "I er – might as well be on my way then."

"Good luck," muttered Johnny. But it was clear that he didn't mean a word of it. His words meant nothing at all, they were just a sop to get rid of Billy. His face was almost scornful as he watched Billy walk away.

He turned back to the side-tunnel as Billy disappeared from view. Johnny was more intent on waiting for Nikki to emerge again.

Chapter Nineteen

There was nothing for Nikki to do but wait for Sarah to wake up, and judging by the way she was lying back snoring her head off, that could still be a little way off. Nikki did a bit of work on her story, trying to find a place in it for Sarah. The problem was, she didn't know what the end would be. She didn't know whether it would end happily, with her friend reunited with Billy, or whether it would all end in tears, at the hands of Stick.

Nikki looked around the den. She'd got it tidied up, and was ready to leave. She hoped her things would still be there when she came back again. She wouldn't like to bet money on it though – you could never be sure down in Underworld; people slipped in as soon as your back was turned. They might steal all her

belongings and she would return to an empty
cave. Maybe she would be able to make another
chapter of her book out of it.

She glanced across at Sarah, who was sleeping
so innocently, with her mouth open and her hair
spilling untidily across her face. She looked as
though she didn't have a care in the world,
except for the creases at the corners of her
mouth. Even in sleep Sarah was still feeling
tense. It seemed unfair that she was having such
problems from a man like Stick. It seemed
unfair that there were men like Stick in the
world.

Nikki looked at her watch. It was late afternoon now, and probably not a good time to be
moving on anyway. She decided to leave Sarah
to sleep. They could move on in the evening,
when the system was quieter, when the com-
muters had all gone home.

She lit another stub of candle to cast a little
extra light on the page. Then she settled down
in her armchair and went back to her book.

But the turning pages made Sarah jerk
awake. "What was that?" she said, nervously.

"What was what?" said Nikki.

"I thought I just heard something."

"It was nothing, only me. You were dreaming, go back to sleep."

Sarah closed her eyes again as Nikki lit a third candle. It chased more of the darkness away, but Nikki felt a shudder inside her as she turned her attention back to the book. There was something outside. She could sense it through the silent air, and she tried not to think about it because it was sometimes best to ignore these things.

But she twitched a little nervously as Sarah plunged into her dream again. Sarah whimpered softly, and Nikki glanced round uneasily.

Even the dog seemed uneasy, as he stared at the canvas door-flap. From time to time he gave a warning growl deep in his throat.

Chapter Twenty

Nikki wasn't the only one with a lot on her mind, Detective Renton had a few problems, too. He'd never spent much time in Underworld before, and it wasn't as straightforward as he'd thought it would be. He was finding it hard to make any real progress.

He'd found a few people, but they hadn't been able to help him, and he was beginning to appreciate just how big the whole system is. It was a nightmare trying to find Stick in that labyrinth.

And the darkness unsettled him, as did the noises drifting out of it, so that Renton felt like a stranger cast ashore on a distant world. He took a glance at this watch. It was only four in the afternoon, though it felt much later. It was hard to keep track of time down there, and he was tired from the hours he'd spent trudging round; but time was short, and he didn't know how much more was left.

The teenagers had been down there for two days, and might drift out again at any time. He had to keep searching; he had to drive Stick on ahead of him. He had to drive him into a corner, and then haul him out again. He gave a sigh as he adjusted the pack on his back.

He didn't know which way to go, but suddenly froze as he heard a sound.

There was somebody groaning ahead of him.

It was a terrible sound, like a beast that's about to die. It made the blood chill inside Renton's veins.

Water was trickling somewhere – he could hear it dripping down the walls, and the echoes of his own footsteps were tossed back into his face. He could feel a breeze drifting down the track, with the stench of decay on it. He thought he saw menacing shadows start to shift on the walls.

He could see a hole up ahead of him, a ragged tear in the tunnel's wall, and out of this came the terrible groaning sound. Renton paused, hearing the sound of his own tight breaths.

Something was calling out mournfully, in

that sepulchral darkness. The detective felt the sweat on his face as he peered inside.

"Are you okay?" he asked quietly.

An old woman looked up at him, grimacing out of a face that was twisted and fissured with lines of pain. Her skin was as dark as the tunnels, but her eyes were almost snowdrop white. She said, "I'm okay. I'm just in some pain, is all."

The detective nodded reassuringly as he advanced into the room. He crouched down beside her and turned up an oil lamp so that its thin, yellow light spilled across the room. It revealed an Aladdin's cave of mystic treasures, and an ancient woman sprawled on a bed of rags. She seemed as big as a dinosaur, and gave him a weary laugh. "Kind of big, ain't I, Mister?"

Renton grinned. "I've seen bigger," he said.

"But not many."

"No, not many," he said, as he bent down to check her pulse.

"I've got a fever," she murmured. "I've laid here for two days all on my own. No one came, till you heard me and walked in through the door."

"You're a bit off the beaten track in this side-tunnel," said the detective. He lay her arm back on top of the rags. "How are you feeling?"

"Pretty rough," she said. "I ain't eaten nothing."

Renton nodded. "I'll get you something to eat. Where's your pain? Is it bad?" he asked.

The woman laughed, and her eyes rolled like spinning tops. "I've got pains about everywhere, but it ain't so bad I'm about to die. It's kind of tolerable, except when I try to move." She tried to sit on the tangled bed, and Renton had to reach down to help her up; the woman didn't have the strength to raise the weight of her body up. "I couldn't get up to eat, or do anything. And that damn fool cat keeps hanging round. I couldn't feed the cat either." She gave another laugh. "Some kind of witch I turned out to be."

Renton smiled as he pulled the covers up over the big woman. "Is that what you are?" he asked. "A witch?"

"Some folk call me that," she said. "I'm the local herb doctor. People come to me when they're feeling sick and I make them up potions. Some of them say they think I'm some kind of witch."

Renton smiled again. "What do you say?" he

asked.

The black woman's shoulders shrugged. "I'm just a woman who likes to help people out. Except when I get sick myself, when I'm just like a little kid. I can't even move, can't do nothing. Can't even get up to feed the cat. I'm too fat, that's the problem — it doesn't help much when you've got to shift this lot around."

"How did you get in this state?"

"Someone pushed me. Deliberately. I twisted my hip up. It's the hip that's been causing me so much pain." The woman patted her fat behind, as if checking on her weight problem. The sound that came back seemed to have a comforting effect on her. "It ain't nothing too serious; I just need to lie and rest up for a while. I've got to draw out the fever, except I can't fix my poultices up. The stupid pain is so bad I can't drag myself out of bed."

Renton nodded again. He adjusted the wick of the sputtering lamp, which had started to cough evil smoke into the gloomy room. "Where's the stuff?" he said, looking round. "I'll make up your poultices."

"It's all over there somewhere, lying round." The woman waved a great hand, about the size of a dustbin lid. "You've got to get some soft rags torn up, and soak them in mould and tea. That's what will do it.''

Renton gave a rather doubtful look. "Where do you get all this stuff?" he asked. "Can't you just take two aspirin with a cup of tea?"

"My mother came from Jamaica, and her mother *was* a proper herbal-witch. Only these days they'd call her a herbalist.'' The woman gave him a knowing look – she thought it was amusing to be called a witch. "And they'd charge you a whole lot of money too. But she knew what she was talking about. I served a proper apprenticeship. I went to a genuine witch's school."

Renton smiled as he stood up and moved across to a cluttered desk. He blew the dust away and said, "Where do I start with all this?" He was faced with about two hundred bottles of various colours, shapes and sizes. It was like the playground of a half-insane alchemist. "Do you really use all this stuff?" he muttered, as he read a few of the handwritten labels. *"Crushed beetles?"*

"Those bugs are magic for clearing spots and boils." The woman rolled herself on to her side and began to direct him with her mighty hand. "But the main thing you should start with, is boiling tea."

Renton put a flame under a huge kettle, big enough to float the *Titanic* in.

"And you can make us some grub while you're hanging round."

Sarah opened her eyes and stirred lazily on the bed. "What's the time?" she said.

Nikki woke with a sudden start. "Crikey, it's almost six o'clock!" she said. "I must have dropped off myself for a while." She looked around and saw her papers strewn across the floor. "I must have—" she clicked her tongue irritably. "All my papers fell on the floor." She leaned down to pick them up and crammed them into a battered folder. "Time's getting on. We should get something to eat, then be on our way."

Sarah nodded. "I feel a lot better," she said. "I think I'm much better now."

"So you should be – you've been snoring like a dying mule." Nikki got to her feet and gave a stretch which made her shoulders crack. She rubbed her face. "I could do with some more sleep myself. But we'd better get moving, 'cause I keep having these funny thoughts. And the dog's acting strangely – he's been padding round a lot."

"Do you think there's somebody out there?" said Sarah, as she swung her legs from a grey blanket. Her hair fell in a mad tangle about her face, like an old, collapsed umbrella.

"I don't know," murmured Nikki. She looked a little strained and uncomfortable. "Sometimes I think I hear things, but maybe I've just lived down here too long. It's probably nothing, or just the sound of wind in the Underground. Or maybe it's rats hunting round for food."

Sarah didn't get too concerned about it. She had a lot of faith in Nikki, and was happy to hand most of the responsibility over to her. After a fortnight of living rough on the city streets, it was nice to have all her decisions taken care of by someone else. Maybe if she had pursued this line of thought a little, she would have come to the realisation that she wasn't yet ready to be living on her own. There's a lot of difference between growing up and *thinking* about growing up. Growing up was something you learned while you were actually doing it.

But at the moment she wasn't thinking about that – she was just content to feel herself safe and warm. "What will we do when we get there?" she asked cheerfully.

"Get to where – Hammersmith?" Nikki shrugged. "I don't know yet, I haven't thought about it." Although she didn't know it, Nikki was faced with the opposite problem; she was the one having to *take* decisions. After two years living on her own, it was a little intimidating. It was hard to cover every contingency. "I, erm – we'll think about it when we get there. Something else might occur to us." That seemed a good way of handling things: put them off for a while. You never knew what might happen – someone else might decide for you. *Never do today what you can put off till tomorrow.*

The older girl took a deep breath. "Right, we'd better get organised. The first thing to do – we'd better get ourselves something to eat." She opened a tin of meat for the dog, and handed Sarah a crumpled-up biscuit packet.

"Is this our dinner?"

"What do you expect?" said Nikki. "It's not the Ritz here – we're living in Underworld."

Sarah took the packet and tugged it open. Nikki's words had a sobering effect; she suddenly realised that it was time to start thinking about things. It was one thing to run away, and quite another to survive out on your own. You left a lot of good things behind when you walked out that door.

"Are you happy?" she asked quietly.

"Yes, I guess so. I'm happy enough."

Sarah nodded. She wasn't sure if she was happy herself.

Nikki seemed to know what she was thinking. She touched her arm reassuringly. "Don't worry, it will be better in the morning, when we're well out of Stick's long reach."

Sarah nodded again. She wasn't sure of that either. All of a sudden, she wasn't too sure of anything.

Jack Renton finally succeeded in making up a poultice that satisfied the black lady's stringent requirements. He thought it smelt like old horse-dung, but the woman seemed quite content with it. She breathed a sigh of contentment as she pressed the damp cloth against her hip. "That's a lot better," she murmured, her eyes closing blissfully.

"Are you sure? You wouldn't rather have a doctor down?"

"I don't trust them doctors," she murmured. "They fill you with drugs and things. This is the real stuff, the *herb* stuff, the naturals."

"There aren't any herbs in it," he muttered. "It's full of bird droppings and rotten moss."

"But at least it's natural."

He couldn't argue about that – she seemed happy enough. Renton pulled up a rickety dining chair which had fallen off the back of a lorry somewhere, and let a long, lazy cat climb on to his lap. It purred with contentment as it stretched its claws and sank them into his thighs. He tried to ignore it as it started pressing its feet up and down. "How long have you been down here?" he asked.

"Oh, eight years, twelve years now. I can't remember," she murmured. "But it seems like a long time ago."

"Don't you ever go up?"

"What's the need?" she said, opening her eyes. She gazed straight up at the ceiling, as if there might have been messages there. "I've got all I need in this neighbourhood. People come to me when they're sick. I've got my cat, got my comfy bed. I've got my fungus, my moulds. What other things I need?"

"It seems a strange kind of life," said Renton.

"That's because you don't understand. You think that life should be motors, and shopping and Hollywood. Down here it's very peaceful, and nobody bothers you."

The way she was staring gave Renton a sudden thought. He moved his chair closer, and peered at her carefully. "Are you blind?" he said.

"Yes, I'm blind," said the black woman.

"How long have you been blind?" he asked.

"Ooh, I guess about – four years." The black woman twisted to smile at him. "I'm Blind Martha, the witch doctor." She laughed with delight at that. She always found that one a terrific joke.

"Isn't it dangerous?" asked Renton. "There's a lot of obstacles in this place."

"It's no more dangerous than trying to walk round the city streets. At least down here you can hear the trains coming towards you."

"But you could have starved to death," said Renton.

The woman shrugged, as though that wasn't too important. "God always seems to take care of me. He always seems to look after me. He sent you to find me, and I can tell that you're a good boy."

"I'm a little more than a boy," he said.

Martha reached out to take his hand, and

gently stroked her rough fingers across his palm. "You're all boys to me," she said. "Everyone's a child to me. Do you know how old I am? Can you tell, just by looking at me?"

"About sixty," said Renton.

"No, I'm seventy-nine years old." Martha smiled again. She had spent the whole of her life giving gentle smiles. "I've had seventy-nine years, and I'm content with the life I've led."

"Except someone pushed you," said Renton. "And nearly broke your hip."

"That's that damn fool Stick," Martha snorted. "Have you ever met him? Do you know him? He's a strange one, he is very bad. He's got total evil trapped inside his veins. I can tell by the way he says his name. The damn fool pushed me out of his way – nearly threw me under a train. That's how I got twisted up. That's how I busted my hip up."

"When was this?" said Renton, suddenly attentive. "When did he do this to you?"

"Oh, I don't know." Martha shrugged her arms carelessly. "Maybe two days ago now, I can't really remember. But he's a bad one – he always brings trouble to life. I used to know him before, when he used to come here for love potions. I said, 'Stick, they don't make potions strong enough!' Not for a bad boy like that. No one loves someone that evil." Martha's eyes twinkled. "But I've got one for you, young man!"

Renton grinned. "I'm okay," he said. "I don't think I need love potions."

"It'll make some girls love you for ever, make 'em love you deep." Martha reached high above her head and fumbled for a phial on a crowded shelf. She used the sleeve of her nightgown to brush off a film of dust. "Give her this," she said, playfully. "Sprinkle this on her Sugar Puffs, and she will love you for ever, she'll be one good love."

Renton smiled as he took the bottle and slipped it into his jacket pocket. "I'll give it a try," he said. "And come back and tell you if it works or not."

"Don't come back for at least thirty years, or it's too soon to tell." The old woman giggled as she thought about it, and shook her great round head with mirth. "Come back in thirty years," she said. "I might still be around the place."

"I hope so," said Renton. And he meant it.

Martha gave a long sigh. "Yes, I might be around." She reached under the bedclothes and groped in a secret bag she kept out of sight.

"Take this as well," she said, taking out a small silver charm. "This is for good luck. It's a talisman, to protect you and keep you safe. You take it with you, and you won't ever come to harm." She slipped it into Renton's cupped hand and said, "What are you doing in this place anyway?"

"Looking for Stick," he said.

"Then you ought to take two of them!" Martha gave a great, hooting laugh, with all the gusto of a younger woman. "But you won't need it, not a good boy like you, I think. But you've got to take care now, because that Stick, he's a wicked one."

"I know," Renton murmured. "I will take care."

"But you've got to take just enough care, because you've got to make sure that you get the man."

"You never get something for nothing," he said quietly.

"That's what I'm telling you. You're a good boy, but don't be too good or it isn't no fun at all!" she cried. "If you act *too* good!" And she laughed like a child, with unrestrained delight.

Renton patted her hand, as he stood up and prepared to resume his search. "Do you need anything more?" he asked.

"Just for you to stay safe and sound."

He nodded. "I'll come back and see you."

"I'm always here waiting." Martha reached up to touch his face. "Just be sure that you take extra care of yourself."

Renton fingered the talisman as he went back into the dark tunnels. With Stick around, he needed all the luck he could get.

Chapter Twenty-one

Johnny looked up. He could hear people coming, their voices preceding them through the
gloom. It was something of a relief, as he'd
grown bored with his solitary vigil, and had
been on the point of giving up on Nikki
Deveraux. The approaching voices were encour-
aging, because he recognised one of them. It
was the voice of his idol; the voice of Stick
Malloy.

Johnny jumped to his feet and ran off
through the gloom like a dog on the scent of
something interesting. He knew that things
happened around Stick, and there were things
to be learned from him. He was a genuine gang-
ster of Underworld.

"Hi, how you doing, Stick?" he said, as he
ran out of the darkness, making Stick jump like

a rabbit, and curse the sudden shock. "I've been hanging around and I heard you two down the track. What you up to? Do you need any help at all?"

"You stupid prat!" muttered Stick. He was tempted to thump him one, but appreciated that he'd been cast in the rôle of a folk hero. You couldn't turn fans away, in case one day you needed them. Even sick ones, like the weasel-faced Johnny D. "What you up to?" he murmured.

But Johnny had already turned away. "Hiya, Nuts," he said cheerfully.

"Push off!" said Nuts.

"What you up to? Are you doing something?"

"We're building a dam," said Nuts.

Johnny frowned. Then he recognised sarcasm. But it didn't deter him, and he fell into step beside them. "Are you planning a job?"

"No, we're looking for dam-builders."

"Oh." Johnny frowned. "I've been waiting for someone, you know – hanging round watching."

"Yeah? That's thrilling." Nuts' sense of boredom was getting the better of him.

"Yeah." Johnny was staring at the ground, as if this made him look more important. He had to lengthen his stride to keep up with them. "I was watching this Nikki. Do you know her?"

"Probably not," said Nuts. Stick was too wrapped up in his own thoughts to even listen to them.

"I think she's been up to something," said Johnny. "So I was keeping an eye on her. I'm good at that, you know – dead good at watching people."

"Yeah?" Nuts couldn't give a monkey's, and a yawn spread across his face. He seemed to have been wandering around Underworld for years now. "You haven't seen a girl wandering round?"

"No. What girl? Are you looking for her?"

"No, I was making polite conversation. What do you think?" said Nuts. "Of course we're looking for her. Why else would I ask if you'd seen her?"

Johnny frowned again. He stared at the ground almost fiercely. "What's she done?" he said, after a while.

"She hasn't done anything that you should know. We're just looking for her. She's been a bit hard to find."

Johnny nodded. He fell thoughtful, giving his attention to the problem. "Maybe Nikki knows something," he said helpfully. "She was buying extra food in, and she was talking to someone. I heard them whispering, like they're both up to something."

Stick stopped abruptly as this information penetrated his wandering thoughts. "Talking to who?" he said quickly. "Who was she talking to?"

Johnny shrugged. "I don't know," he said. "Just back there – she was talking to someone. She wouldn't let me near her den. She kept the door closed and wouldn't let me in."

"Was she talking to a girl?" asked Stick, cautiously.

"Yeah, I guess so," said Johnny, suddenly becoming aware that they were watching him closely. It was a little intimidating to be stared at; he wished he'd kept his big mouth shut.

"Just back there?" said Stick.

"Yeah. In one of those side-tunnels."

Stick looked at Nuts. "What do you think?" he said. "Do you think that's her?"

Nuts shrugged his shoulders. "How do I know? It could have been anyone."

"But I've got a feeling," said Stick. "I've got

a feeling about it." A grin spread over his face as he touched Nuts on the shoulder. "I bet that's her. You'd better show me the way, Kid."

Things suddenly seemed a great deal better. Johnny could see that Stick was feeling pleased with him. He beamed. "Sure. Hey, my name's Johnny, by the way."

Stick wasn't interested in that. All he wanted to do was check out this new lead. He almost threw Johnny down the dark tracks ahead of him.

"Right, we'd better get going," said Nikki, "before we waste any more time." She grabbed hold of the last bag, which contained all the foodstuff.

"What about your book and things?" said Sarah. "Are you going to leave your book behind?"

Nikki frowned as she looked at the heaps of paper scattered across the floor.

"I suppose I'd better take it," she murmured. "You never know who might wander in. I might get some nutter who wants to set fire to things." She dropped to her knees and started to gather the pages up, trying to make some order out of a scene like a paper chase.

Sarah wandered to the doorway to glance out while she was waiting. As she pulled the canvas screen back, she heard voices approaching. She froze as she recognised one of them. . . .

Chapter Twenty-two

"They've gone," Stick said disgustedly, as he burst in on Nikki's empty den like a bull charging into a china shop. "The place is empty — you've brought us on a wild goose chase." He kicked over the desk.

Johnny stared around dismally; he couldn't believe that the girls had somehow slipped away.

"They were right here a minute ago," he said. "I could hear them talking. They were in here—"

"So where are they now?" said Stick. He was spitting with fury, his thin face white with rage.

"I don't know," Johnny murmured, and could feel himself turning pale. "They must have sneaked out." He had a sinking feeling in his guts.

Stick wasn't pleased with Johnny's answer. He considered making this plain to him in the way he knew best, then changed his mind and started ripping up the furniture. Taking a knife from his pocket, he slashed it into the mattress and stabbed it deep into a bundle of Nikki's clothes. "What are they doing now?" he said, snarling, as Johnny D. backed away from him. "Are they hiding in the walls or something?"

"Take it easy," said Nuts quietly. "They can't be that far away."

Stick gave a growl. "He's full of crap!" he cried, as he tore Nikki's posters down, and ripped all her papers into shreds.

"It wasn't his fault—"

"It wasn't *my* fault!" Stick whirled around angrily. He was panting with fury, his hands bunched into knuckled fists. "I'm going to kill him," he muttered. "I'm going to kill someone." Almost dementedly he pulled the den apart, hurling Nikki's few possessions outside on to the tracks, breaking her wooden chairs up, smashing the crockery. He was like a creature gone wild.

Nuts had seen Stick like this before – he had seen Stick lose his self-control. There wasn't anything to do except wait until the rage burned down. But it was a dangerous time, because he was liable to turn it on Nuts himself. Or maybe Johnny. Nuts tried to steer the youngster safely through the door.

"Hey, they can't be that far away," he said, "if they've only just left the place. Why don't we go look for them? They might even be coming back—"

Stick paused.

"Yeah, you're right," he said, taking deep breaths to calm his racing heart. "They could still be around. We should split up and look for them. Maybe they've just wandered off somewhere, down the tracks."

He put his hands on the wall while he continued to breathe deeply. He was trying to think; he wasn't brainless, he could handle this.

"We could go different ways," he said, panting the words out. "Take a tunnel each and if you find them, call the others back. Tap on the rails with a rock or a lump of wood. Sound goes for miles here; just give it three heavy taps. And when you hear that, come back here, and we'll know which way we have to go. Have you got that?" The others nodded. "Okay, let's get moving. Don't let them see you till I get there.

I'm going this way—" Without any further comment, Stick disappeared off along the track.

The other two waited a few moments in the sudden pool of silence that remained. They were still feeling shaken by Stick's maniacal outburst.

Nuts finally managed to stir himself. "Which way do you want to go?" he said, quietly.

"Erm—" Johnny tried to shift his mind into gear again. "I'll er, maybe go this way."

"Yeah. Keep out of his way," said Nuts, "if he ever gets like that again."

There wasn't any need to say that; Johnny had already decided. He couldn't wait to leave Nikki's devastated den.

They trotted off down their respective tunnels, while silence filled up Nikki's empty den. It was a silence so complete, it might never be swept away again.

Chapter Twenty-three

The two girls stopped, panting for breath, having put a good distance between themselves and Stick. They didn't think he was following them, or even that he'd caught a glimpse of them, but it had been a close call, and it was worrying. It was worrying that he had been able to sneak up so close to them. It was worrying that he knew where they were. It was something they didn't want to think about in case it made Stick seem supernatural. It was hard enough being hunted by a mortal man.

Sarah gave a shudder, and then a gasp as she suddenly remembered something. "What about Billy?" she said, dismayed that she'd forgotten him.

Nikki was still panting, bending forward with her hands on her knees. She didn't look up as she said, "It's okay, I've already thought of that." She straightened slowly, pressing her hands against the small of her back.

"How is he going to find us?" cried Sarah.

"We'll leave him directions. We do this kind of thing all the time." Nikki stuck a hand into her jacket pocket and pulled out a length of dusty chalk. She brushed some fluff off it. "I'll write up some messages. He can follow us to Hammersmith, and we'll meet up with him when he gets down there."

She stepped over the live rail and reached up to scrawl across the wall. In big bold letters she scribbled:

BILLY – GONE TO HAMMERSMITH.

She wrote an *S* after it. "I can't write it any bigger than that. If he can't read it, there's something wrong with his eyesight."

"What if Stick sees it?" asked Sarah.

"You said he never asked you what your names are. It won't mean anything to him – there are messages all over the place. People use the walls as notice boards." Nikki drew an arrow to show which way Billy should go. "Easy-peasy," she said.

"Easy-peasy, lemon squeezy." Sarah gave a grin. It was good to leave Stick behind. She felt a great sense of relief that they were finally under way. It had been a close thing when he missed them, but all they needed now was a little luck. With a little luck, they'd be in Hammersmith by morning.

Twenty minutes later Johnny D. spotted them, on the Piccadilly line southbound, half-way between Piccadilly Circus and Green Park. He was keeping close to the wall, advancing as fast as he could. He heard their laughter long before he saw them.

He was good at creeping up on people, and could move like a cat at times. Sometimes he believed he could make himself invisible. He advanced until he could see them by the lights from the signal lamps.

When he was sure it was them, Johnny began to crawl backwards, and when he was out of sight, he looked around for a lump of rock. He couldn't find one, but instead picked up a piece of old metal. He used that to beat the three notes upon the rails. The din was louder than he expected, and the sound almost deafened him as it rang on and on through the tunnel system. It rolled on for kilometres, and was picked up by

Stick's ears. He gave a grin of dark triumph as he turned back towards the sound.

It was just what Stick needed; a change of fortune in his recent spell of lousy luck. He grunted savagely as he began his trek back to Nikki's den.

He met Nuts at the entrance, and they started to run to catch up with Johnny.

The hunters were closing in rapidly on Sarah now.

"What was that?" said Nikki curiously, turning to stare back down the ringing shaft. "It sounds like a steel band. Maybe someone got lost down here."

She retraced her steps a short way, trying to peer through the clinging gloom. "There's someone down there – it's Johnny D. What in Heaven's name's he doing?" She screwed her eyes up, trying to penetrate the shade, but could see only Johnny's outline, crouching on the tracks.

"He's looking down this way – what's he playing at? I think he must have gone crazy. He's hopping around like a rat." She still couldn't see Johnny too clearly – he was almost hidden by a curve in the wall, and deep shadows were strewn across him like camouflage. "He's a weird one," she muttered. Then she shrugged, and walked back down the track.

Sarah was trying hard to peer past her at the figure of the skulking boy. "What's he making that noise for?"

"God knows," said Nikki. "He's totally crazy. Still, it isn't any of our concern."

The girls picked up their bags again and proceeded along the empty tracks. They had no idea of the danger which was closing in on them from behind.

Chapter Twenty-four

"Hello?" Billy said hopefully, as he peered into a side-tunnel. He thought he heard something rustling inside the velvet depths.

The sound immediately stopped, and he crept forward cautiously. "Is anyone there?" he said.

His own voice echoed back at him.

Billy paused for a moment to pick up his confidence, but felt more nervous as the still air gathered round him. He felt lonely and vulnerable, silhouetted by the glow of a lamp in the shaft behind. He found himself crouching instinctively into a fighter's stance.

There was a terrible silence, which seemed to be taunting him. "Is someone there?" he said, and wished he'd stayed on the track outside.

"Sarah?" he said, hopefully.

"Sarah ain't here, son. There's nobody in here but weirdoes."

Billy's heart froze inside his chest. He opened his mouth to let out a shout, but nothing emerged but the thinnest of stifled squeals.

Something moved in the darkness, and a hand clutched at Billy's leg.

"What do you want?" he screamed, and tried to run, but his scared legs let him down.

A soft voice answered him pleasantly. "I don't know," it said thoughtfully. "I don't know exactly what it is that you're offering, son."

Nikki glanced back again, and a wary frown spread across her face. "He's there again," she said. "What's he up to? It's like he's following us."

Sarah stood on tiptoe beside her, trying to peer through the gloom. She put her hand on Nikki's shoulder to give herself some support. "I can't even see him," she murmured. "I don't know who we're looking at. Where is he?"

"Over there," said Nikki, quietly. She pointed at the darkness, but Sarah still couldn't see anything. "He's gone into hiding behind that heap of wire."

"What heap of wire?" muttered Sarah, who still couldn't see anything.

"There's a big heap of wire there – some old signal wire behind that great lump of rock."

That didn't help Sarah. All she could see were long pools of grey shadow – her eyes had barely made adjustments to Underworld's shiftless light. But she could hear something rustling, something scrabbling, something small and light. "Maybe he's playing games," she said, hopefully. "He could be fooling around."

"I don't think so – he's watching us." Nikki was standing on tiptoe herself now, trying to see exactly what Johnny was playing at. "He's a weird kid," she muttered, as she squinted even harder. Then she froze for a moment. Her look was horrified.

"Oh my God, he's got Stick with him! He's got Stick coming, right behind! Oh my God, Sarah, run – they're coming after us!"

Nikki dropped all her bags and hurtled off down the silent track, Sarah sprinting after her.

Nikki tossed a glance over her shoulder, as the dog bounded excitedly around her feet. "He's coming, Sarah, Stick's coming! He's after us!"

A group of men stood in a circle, watching Billy bawl and blubber uncontrollably, with all the dignity of a small, lost child.

"What's the matter with him?" said one, totally mystified.

"Oh, not much – you just frightened the life out of him."

"*What* did I do?" said the first voice.

"You only grabbed hold of his leg, didn't you? I mean, look at him—" said a second man, who was built like a brick outhouse. "He's just a kid, and you go fooling round with him."

"I was only fooling," said the first man, putting on an indignant and innocent look.

The other men backed him up in his protest. "He was only fooling round," they said.

"Yeah, I know, but you frightened him. Poor little basket. Come on, kid, it's all right – we're not going to do anything." The second man put his hand on Billy's shoulder, which made him jump out of his skin. The other men looked away in embarrassment. Billy was quite a wreck.

"We were only playing cards," said the second man. "That's what we do." He glanced over his shoulder. "Strike a light, will you? Put some light on the scene. Put the kid at ease, you bunch of morons."

There was a clumsy shuffling of feet, a thin, yellow flame appeared, and someone held it to the wick of a battered oil lamp. A smoky circle of light spread out and lit up a small, dusty cave in the rock. "Look, we were just playing cards," said the man, indicating a green cloth on the floor. "It's just a card school, that's all – it ain't nothing more weird than that—"

"But you were playing in the dark!" said Billy, blurting the words out. He wiped his face on the back of his hand. "I thought you were – I don't know what I thought."

"It can get pretty weird down here. Especially with morons like him around!" The man grinned as he pointed to the tallest of the group, a man so tall he had to stoop to keep from bashing his head in. "It's not so bad when you get used to it. In fact, the light's pretty painful. Will somebody turn that thing down a bit?"

Someone adjusted the flame, and it settled down to a muted glow, though the cave was still as dark as midnight to Billy's frightened eyes. A man threw his coat on the floor and tried to get the youngster to sit on it, but he was so locked-up in his tension, he couldn't bend enough. Instead he slumped against the wall.

"You scared me to death!" he said accusingly, his hands shaking. "I thought you might have been werewolves – or anything!"

The second man started to laugh. "We're just a bunch of old men," he said. "We only come here to play cards, and get drunk and stagger home, and if our wives find out what we're up to, there's going to be hell to pay. That's the only reason we come down here, to get away from the old buggers. We've come down here for years, we've worn grooves where we rest our feet."

While the old man was talking, the others had returned to their card table, and were settling themselves down on the floor again. The old man could see that Billy had some problems, and took him to one side to have a word with him. He'd raised four sons of his own, and knew how hard life was.

"Sit down there," he said quietly, indicating a shelf set into the wall. He helped Billy on to it, clambered after him, and gave a gentle burp. He took an old bottle from his jacket pocket, wiped his hand round the grimy rim, and thrust it decisively into Billy's hand. "You just take a good swig on that, son."

Billy raised the bottle to his lips, and a blast of neat vodka almost burned the roof of his mouth off. His eyes started watering as he passed the bottle back. "I've never had anything as strong as that before," he gasped. "I've only had lager."

"Aye, it's rough stuff, I make it myself in an old tin bath." The old man poured a draught down his own throat, and burped again happily. "It's good stuff. It takes paint off. Does everything."

Billy felt himself grow warm almost instantly as the vodka roared through his stunned insides. Then he remembered, and tears rose in his eyes.

"I've been walking for hours," he said dismally. "I've been wandering all over the place. I couldn't find anyone, or see anything, and I kept hearing things. There are things in the distance, you know, making all kinds of sounds. But you can't see them, and it sounds like there's ghosts."

The old man nodded sympathetically, as he passed the half-empty bottle back. "Aye, they do say there are ghosts wandering round the place. But I don't think you should worry – no one ever got killed by ghosts. They might frighten the wits out of you, but they don't creep up and slip their hands round your throat."

That wasn't the right thing to say. It was things like that which kept Billy awake at night.

"I got—" Billy gave a short burp himself and took another swig from the vodka bottle. "I got scared, and I got lonely, and I'm completely lost."

"Easy done," said the old man, taking the bottle back for a good long slug.

"Yeah, I know," muttered Billy, as he waited for his turn.

"Aye." The old man stared off into space, as if he was trying to imagine a world seen through Billy's eyes, trying to remember what it must have been like when he first came into Underworld. He'd been down there so long he could hardly remember it; it was only when he went topside that he started to get upset.

"I got married down here," he murmured, drifting away on dreams. "I got married for the second time, after my first wife died. That was when I came down here, when Sheila went. Because I—" his words suddenly dried up on him, as he forgot what he was talking about. Then it came back with a rush, and he rambled on again.

"Oh, yeah – I cracked up when she died, and I came to live down here, and made some new friends, and I've lived here for fifteen years. I got married to Ada—" That made him shake his head dismally. He took the bottle back and poured down another slug. "Blooming Ada. What a woman she turned out to be."

Billy was beginning to loosen up a little. His head was warmer, his eyes were turning soft. He was enjoying the sensation of the vodka working round his brain. He could actually plot the course it was taking as he felt it sweep through his weary cells. His mouth dropped open as he peered vaguely through the gloom.

The old man was watching the bottle, as though he'd never seen one close up before. "It's one of the strongest drinks you can make," he said. "I make it all myself."

"It's pretty good," murmured Billy. He threw his head back and took a long, noisy drink. "It's kind of – really, I think it's quite good really."

The man nodded. "I know what you mean. Anyway, Ada—" he started to sway a little, and put his hand on Billy's shoulder to steady himself. "She's a tyrant," he muttered. "She's a flaming witch. I should have never got married to her. I think I was drunk, I think. She gets me to do all the washing up. All the cleaning. I do *everything*." He sounded very upset about it. He put his arm round Billy's other shoulder, and tried hard to peer straight into Billy's eyes. "Don't you ever do that, son. Don't you ever get married again."

"I haven't been married yet," said Billy. He didn't think he had.

"Oh." The old man had to spend a little time thinking about that. It seemed like kind of a problem for him. After a while he said, "Well, don't get married anyway."

"No. I'm looking for my girlfriend."

The old man nodded. They were big mates now. There was nothing like getting drunk, for turning into two life-long friends. "And does she drink?" he murmured.

"I don't think so," said Billy.

"Ah. In that case, you ought to forget her then." The old man started to laugh. "Why don't we open another bottle?" and he fell off the ledge as gravity suddenly defeated him.

Billy sat a while looking at him, then fell off

the ledge himself. The last thing he remembered was the chamber swirling round his head.

"They're gaining on us!" yelled Sarah. "They're catching us!" She put on a spurt as she heard Stick shouting. He was flying like the wind, cutting down their lead. In the echoing tunnel, the sound of his footsteps was like gunshots bouncing back off the iron-ringed walls. They seemed to be battering Sarah, drowning out her own footsteps so that she wasn't sure if she was simply running or lost in a dreadful dream. All she could see was the darkness and faint lights flickering ahead of her. She could hardly see Nikki for the wind lashing at her eyes.

"He's right behind us!" she cried.

Nikki turned to take a look behind, and in that moment lost her footing. She tripped over the dog, which was bounding between her legs, and pitched forward on the track with a startled cry.

Sarah stopped. "Are you all right?" she said, stooping to help Nikki up.

"Yeah, I think so," Nikki said, wincing at the pains shooting down her leg. She started limping as she struggled at Sarah's side.

"He's getting closer," said Sarah.

Nikki grunted, and took another look back. "We've got to lose him. We've got to get out of sight for a while. Get up there," she panted.

"Get up where?"

"Up those steps in the wall."

Sarah couldn't see a thing. "Get up where?"

"Up those steps!" cried Nikki. She pushed Sarah ahead of her. "There's some steps, there's some steps in the wall. They go up to an air-shaft—"

Sarah looked at her doubtfully. "Will you be able to make it?"

"What — with my leg? I don't know. We haven't got much choice. You'll have to carry me if I can't — we can't hang around down here."

"What about Sam?"

Nikki sighed. "All these problems! We don't have time to worry about them! You just start climbing, and I'll pass him up to you." She bit on her lip. There wasn't time to feel pain now. Stick would be coming soon. . . .

Chapter Twenty-five

There was no room to move. The girls had crawled along the air-shaft as far as they could go and were now crammed in like sardines with the dog shivering between them, caught up in their fear. Two metres below, Stick was pounding on down the track; they could have reached down and touched him. He had missed them by moments, but didn't hear them slide a metal grille into place. If he had paused to listen, he would have heard their short, panted breaths.

But Stick charged by like a lunatic, with Johnny and Nuts trailing in his wake, and as all three rushed on madly through the darkness, a wary peace returned. It was the kind of peace that said the danger wasn't over by a long chalk. It was the kind of silence that seemed to say that Stick wasn't an idiot, and it wouldn't take him long to think of doubling back.

"What are we going to do?" whispered Sarah.

"Double back and find another way."

"Do you think he'll find us?"

"I don't know, but we can't give up." Nikki grabbed hold of Sarah's arm, and as she moved a burning pain lanced down her leg. "We're like rats in a trap here – we have to get out."

"I don't want to move," muttered Sarah.

"Neither do I, but we must go." Nikki tried to be reassuring, but didn't sound too convinced herself. The matter had gone beyond an adventure, and it was clear that Stick was intent on running the two girls down. It was not a game now, and their lives depended on staying out of reach. "We have to go while we can," said Nikki. "Before he comes back and checks up here."

Sarah nodded tensely. "Are you scared?"

"Yes, I'm scared to death." Nikki slid back the metal grille and shuffled forward on her belly until she could look outside. She could see only the tracks trailing off into a distant gloom. The empty tunnel was silent, except for an occasional shout from the hunting gang. "Get out now, while you can. I'll be right behind."

Sarah peered down at the drop. It didn't look

too inviting. "It's a long way," she said. "If we botch it, we could break our necks."

"He'll break our necks if he catches us, and we haven't got time to make a rope. Go on. I'll be right behind."

Sarah swung her legs over the edge and began to wriggle out backwards. Then she paused. "What should I do if he grabs my leg?"

"Kick him hard in the teeth," said Nikki. "And I'll drop the dog on his head."

Sarah grinned. "You're insane."

"Not as daft as you."

Sarah slithered through the gap, and rested her weight on her elbows. She waved her feet around, trying to find something to brace them on. "I hope you know what you're doing," she said.

"I've got the whole thing figured out. If he catches you, I'm going to stay up here on my own!"

"We must've lost them," said Stick. He stared ahead down the empty tracks at the glow of lights burning at Green Park station. There was no way the girls could have got there without Stick catching up with them. "They must have doubled back somewhere, gone down a side-tunnel."

"We didn't pass one," said Nuts, glancing back over his shoulder. He couldn't see any side-tunnels nor any off-shoots, and they had not passed a fork.

Stick shrugged his shoulders. "It doesn't matter," he said. "They must still be round here somewhere. We can find them now, because we can seal this whole section off." Now that he was close, a chilling calm had settled over Stick, as if he were saving up all his fury until he had the girls. Nuts had never seen him like that before, and it was even more unsettling than his usual moods. At least you knew who he was when he was blowing his top.

"We'll walk back slowly," Stick murmured, "and keep our eyes peeled for any tracks. There might be a hidden air-shaft or something, or a maintenance path." He patted Nuts on the shoulder, and Nuts almost flinched from the deathly touch. "Don't worry, Nuts, we're going to find them. It'll be over soon."

"Yeah, sure, Stick," said Nuts cautiously, as if he didn't know what to trust any more. Over-all, he thought he preferred the demented Stick to this one with his unholy calm.

"Yeah, it'll be over soon," Stick repeated, gazing down the empty tunnel with a strangely vacant look in his eyes. "But we'd better move off the tracks now. There's a train coming."

"I've got my belt stuck!" said Sarah, as her legs thrashed madly in the tunnel's air. She was caught half in and out of the small air-duct. "I've got my shirt stuck as well." She found herself trapped on two protruding bolts. She tried to drag herself back again, but the weight of her legs made that difficult. Suspended by her elbows, she couldn't move up or down. After a time she stopped struggling and took a long, deep breath. Her efforts had turned her face pink, and she grinned with embarrassment. "I've got myself stuck. I feel like a fly in a spider's web."

Nikki tried to reach to assist her, but there wasn't a lot of room in the narrow shaft. "Shuffle this way."

"I'm trying to." Sarah turned bright red. "It's my belt," she said, wriggling. "I can't get my hand on it, I'm too fat."

"I'm glad it was you who said that." Nikki struggled to haul her back. She got a grip on

Sarah's shoulders, but there was no room to brace herself. "Maybe you should go on a diet," she said, grunting.

"I would, but there isn't time." Sarah started to grin again. She was stuck so fast, she had no idea what to do. "Do you think he'd notice if he came back and saw my legs waving in the air?"

Nikki started giggling herself, and then suddenly lost control as both girls collapsed into laughter. It was like a wave rushing over them, and once they'd started they couldn't stop. They were helpless with laughter. It forced the breath from them.

"We have to do something quick," said Nikki. "He'll be coming back any minute." But they were having hysterics – they couldn't have stopped if someone paid them to.

"It's not funny, it's hurting! Don't make me laugh, I'll never get away." As Sarah said that, Nikki gave a great hooting roar. There were tears on Sarah's cheeks as her legs thrashed about helplessly. "I've got a pain in my side! *Ow*, it's killing me!"

But even as they were laughing, Sarah sensed something through the air. It made her pause in her merriment. "What was that?" she said.

"What was what?" said Nikki, puzzled.

Sarah frowned. "I thought I heard something. Can't you hear it? Something hissing."

Nikki bent down to listen, straining hard to pick up the sound. Then she felt a faint rumbling coming through the rock. "There's a train coming," she said quietly, as the laughter froze on her face. "You've got to get out of there quick – a train's on its way."

Sarah gave a tense laugh. "But I'm stuck," she said nervously. "My belt's stuck, my shirt's stuck—" She gave another laugh, but it wasn't a good one, it was hardly a real laugh at all. Her legs kicked at the air.

"You've got to get out of there quick, Sarah!" Nikki grabbed her shoulders and tried to pull her back into the small air-shaft.

Sarah could feel thunder approaching, and the whole tunnel shook with it. "It'll break my legs!" she screamed desperately. "It's going to break my legs!"

The train was coming closer and closer, wind roaring on ahead of it. The air was crackling and hissing like overheated fat. Sarah screamed as she tried to drag herself back through the narrow gap, and Nikki grunted and gasped as she hauled at her. The dog was going crazy in the air-shaft, barking and scrabbling.

"It's coming!" screamed Sarah. "It's coming, I can hear the train!" She was turning purple from her efforts, but was still stuck fast. "I'll never make it, I can't move." She looked up at Nikki. Her fingers were locked round the muscles of Nikki's arms.

"I can't make it," she whispered, as Nikki stared at her helplessly. "I'll never make it."

The two girls screamed as the deadly train bore down.

Chapter Twenty-six

Sarah's scream was drowned out by the roar of the train, and Stick didn't notice it as he glanced round impatiently. "What's that?" he said, curiously.

"It's just a message," said Nuts, following his gaze. "It says 'BILLY – GONE TO HAMMERSMITH'. It doesn't mean anything." They were staring up at a wall, where white letters stood out bold and bright. "It's signed by someone called 'S'. It's just a notice board."

It didn't mean anything to Stick and he started to move away, but Johnny stood for a while staring at the sign. He was trying to cast his mind back to something, trying to remember something he had heard. "A lad I met—" he said, "he said his name was Billy. He was down here trying to find someone, looking for somebody. Yeah, his girlfriend. He said his name was Billy."

Stick suddenly paused in mid-stride. He stared ahead down the empty track.

"What did he look like?"

"Just some kid with brown curly hair." Johnny shrugged like it didn't matter. "He was a new guy, he didn't seem to know much about living down here. He had a funny accent—"

"It's him," Stick said quietly. He turned back towards them, still keeping deadly calm. "It's the kids we're looking for." His eyes were cold and dead, like the ashes of a fire that had long burned out. "That's who we're looking for, and they're going towards Hammersmith."

"Are you sure?" said Nuts.

"Who else is it going to be?"

Nuts looked around the tunnel. "But which way would they go?" he asked.

"They'd go the quickest way, straight down the Piccadilly line. If we send someone ahead, we can trap them between us. If someone goes to South Kensington, they can work their way back again." A sudden fire had returned to his eyes. He was looking straight at Nuts. "You go back down the track. About two hundred metres back there's a maintenance door leading to the street. You can get a taxi to Kensington and work your way this way. We'll meet you."

Nuts nodded unhappily. He'd had enough of this whole enterprise. His only hope was that at least it might all be over soon. "What do I do?" he said.

"Nothing, you just keep moving this way. We should trap them somewhere around Knightsbridge. But if you happen to find them, you keep them till I get there. It's the girl I'm after, but I'll sort out that lad as well."

Nuts nodded again as he began to walk slowly down the track.

"And get a move on – we haven't got all day!" said Stick irritably.

Chapter Twenty-seven

Sarah hung limply from the air-shaft as the train disappeared down the tracks, amazed that she still had her legs. At the last second she had swung them up, and felt them bounce off the roof of the thundering train below. She would have heard the sound of their drumming, if her screams hadn't drowned it out.

It knocked all the strength from her and she couldn't move for a long time, but then she looked up, into Nikki's face. "Tell me something," she said. "What are we coming down this way for? Why didn't we go back the same way we came up?"

Nikki glanced over her shoulder and peered back down the air-shaft. "Oh, yeah. I never thought of that," she said. "Why didn't you say something earlier?"

Sarah gave a long sigh. "I thought you knew what you were doing," she said.

"Who, me? No, I make it up as we go along."

Sarah loosened her belt and dropped on to the track below. A few moments later, the dog fell on top of her.

Billy was still staggering from the effects of the vodka when he saw Nikki's sign scribbled on the wall. He was staggering so much he had to sit down to read it, and even then had problems actually deciphering it.

BILLY – GONE TO HAMMERSMITH.

"That's me," he said, puzzled. He looked up to read the sign again.

But he'd lost control of his eyeballs – they were focusing on a patch of rather sea-sick, swirling air. Standing up, he hobbled closer to the sign, took out his torch and aimed it at the white lettering. It ought to mean something, but at that moment he couldn't quite work out what it was. It wasn't easy to think straight with a load of alcohol churning round his veins. He shook his head, but that only made him feel worse. He sat down before he fell down.

Billy shone his torch on the tunnel wall

again, trying to hold the beam steady, but it bounced around like a wand in a whirlwind. He took a deep breath. "Who's 'S'? Oh – it's Sarah," he murmured. "She's left me a message. She's gone on to Hammersmith. Where's Hammersmith?" He looked around like an idiot.

Then he saw the arrow underneath the sign. "Oh – she left me an arrow." He put his face against the wall and tried to squint down the arrow. "I can't see anything—" But the sign was beginning to make sense to him. It was a slow business, but the message was finally getting through to him.

He gave a burp. "She's down that way."

Scrambling to his feet, Billy picked up his bag and fumbled with the torch, and as its light went out he wove unsteadily along the empty tracks. He had to get down to Hammersmith; he had to meet up with Sarah – with any luck they'd be in Milton Keynes by midnight. As long as he didn't do anything stupid, like putting his foot on the live rail, or breaking his neck, or toppling under a train. It seemed a lot to ask, at that moment, as he felt himself bounce off the tunnel walls.

Never again, he thought. *I will never touch vodka again.*

Chapter Twenty-eight

Nuts never really knew what he saw when he opened the door to the maintenance tunnel; it could have been a cat, or a rat, or a half-dead bird. But it frightened the life out of him as it shot out, sending him shrieking and stumbling across the tracks. He hit his head on the wall and toppled sideways at the sudden shock. A long, searing pain streaked down his neck.

The tunnel seemed to lurch, and Nuts reached out to steady himself, but his legs collapsed. He hit his head again, and a giddiness came over him. There was a thud as he fell.

He was sitting on the tracks, and didn't know how he'd got there. He felt sick, and there was a numbing pain at the back of his head. When he put his hand up, he felt blood, and his eyes tried to focus on it. But it was getting difficult, because darkness was closing in on him.

He managed a step on his knees, then pitched headlong on the musty track. He tasted oil before he passed out completely.

Nuts lay for a long time before he began to recover. Slowly, like someone crawling out of a dream, he put his hands down at his sides and tried to raise himself off the dirt.

He did his best, but couldn't lift his head for the pounding pain in it. Someone was beating on a drum, and he had to pause to rest for a moment. He tried to look up, but couldn't clear the haze from his eyes.

All he was aware of was the track a few centimetres in front of him, and the vibration of something grumbling in his chest. It quickly spread to his arms, and then ran down his shaking legs, like a small motor was inside him.

There was something beating the earth, getting closer and closer, making the iron-banded walls of the tunnel shake. He had heard the sound many times before; it was the strident rattle of a speeding train. And Nuts was sprawled out in its path, helpless on the tracks.

He tried to clear the fog from his mind, but still felt barely conscious; he couldn't get his legs to move, he couldn't raise himself off the ground. He was too tired and too stunned, and couldn't make himself think clearly. He knew he had to do something, but wasn't sure what.

He put his hand on the rail. It was cold, and seemed to chill his bones. He tried to haul himself sideways, but couldn't find the strength. He was confused by the train's lights, which were closing in, dazzling him. He put a hand up, and tried to protect his eyes.

The noise was growing louder and louder till the whole passageway was thrumming with it. Nuts could feel his thoughts coming back to him, but not quickly enough. He knew he was in some kind of danger, and rolled on his back while he thought about it. There was a train coming, that was it; and he was in its path . . .

It was beginning to make sense, and at the last moment Nuts realised.

But it was too late by then. The train was already bearing down on him.

Chapter Twenty-nine

Jack Renton propped Nuts against a wall, and forced him to take a swig of brandy from the hip-flask he carried in his coat. He felt his forehead for fever, and checked the frightened youth's pulse-rate. "That was a close call," he said. "You want to be a bit more careful."

Nuts opened his eyes slowly. "What happened?" he said.

"I had to drag you out of the way of a train."

"Bloomin' 'eck!" Nuts let his eyes close exhaustedly. Then he took a deep breath. "I hate it down here," he said, and the next moment began trembling uncontrollably.

All the fear of the last few days came galloping back to Nuts, and his whole body shook with convulsive sobs. He felt like an unwanted child, and couldn't stop himself crying. "I want to go home again! I don't ever want to come back here. It's going to kill me – I know it is. I'll die if I stay down here!" He was getting over-excited, and Renton put a hand on his face again.

"Take it easy," he murmured. "You'll be okay now."

"Yeah." Nuts didn't seem convinced. He was still confused by the blow to the back of his head. "I'll be all right," he said doubtfully, glancing back down the empty tracks. It was as if he was expecting someone to emerge from the threatening gloom.

"Do you have any friends here?" said Renton.

Nuts snorted. "Any friends?" he said. "Are you kidding? You don't make friends in Underworld." He was growing hysterical, and his voice rose alarmingly. A flush like a fever spread across his cheeks.

"Take it easy," Renton said again.

"That's easy for you to say! You don't know what's going on here. I'm probably going to be hauled up for murder!" Before Nuts could help himself, he took a tight hold on Renton's arm. "He's going to *kill* me if I let him down – do you think that's a friend, or what? I think he's some kind of a lunatic." Nuts' expression became frantic; he looked desperate as all the colour drained from his face. His eyes hunted around feverishly, without seeing anything. "He goes crazy. I think he really is mad sometimes."

"Who is?" said Renton, wrapping his jacket round Nuts' shoulders. Nuts was shivering like a leaf on a tree in an autumn gale.

"Flaming Stick!" shouted Nuts. "He goes crazy — he loses all control."

Renton paused a moment. He said, "Is he still around here?"

Nuts jerked a nod. He was confused. "Yeah, you know him?"

"I've heard of him. In fact, I've come down here to try to arrest him."

That one almost slew Nuts. He gawped. "To arrest him? Are you a copper?" Without even thinking about it, he dried to drag himself up the wall.

"I'm a detective," said Renton.

Nuts stopped, and stared suspiciously. "You don't look like one."

Renton smiled. "How am I supposed to look?"

"I don't know. Not that scruffy — you look worse than Stick does." Nuts tied to get a grip on himself, he was in danger of losing his self-control. He ran a hand over his face and took a deep breath. He glanced up to see Renton staring down at him.

"What have *I* done?" said Nuts. "What are you looking at me like that for? I'm not doing anything, I'm just going towards Hammersmith. And I don't even want to, I want to go home again—"

"Did Stick send you?"

"Yeah, I'm supposed to get hold of someone." Nuts was trying to think through the situation, and it was giving him a headache. He put his hand rather gingerly on to Renton's arm. "Hey, listen," he said. "If Stick got arrested, this whole thing would be over and done with. Except—" he paused, as he thought of something. "You might bang me up, too."

"Why, what have you done?" said Renton.

"Nothing! I haven't done anything." Nuts tried to cast his mind back, to see if he had done anything too illegal; but all he could think about was getting well out of Underworld. "I don't think I've done anything," he said.

"Then you've got nothing to worry about." Renton put his hand on Nuts' brow again. Nuts was growing calmer.

"Yeah, right. I haven't done anything." Nuts frowned as he tried to work out the business of getting Stick off his back and walking off scot-free himself. "Hey — if I haven't done anything," he said, trying to choose his words carefully, "If I haven't done anything—"

"Then you've nothing to worry about."

"Yeah, right." Nuts agreed with that, though he thought there could be a catch in it somewhere. The pain in his head was making it hard for him to think clearly. But he hadn't done anything, so what was he worrying about? He could dump Stick now, before things got any more out of hand.

Renton sat down beside him. He pulled a muesli bar and a well-travelled can of Coke out of his rucksack, and gave them to Nuts. He found a bar for himself and sat chewing on it thoughtfully. He was hoping Nuts would say something more.

"Are you in Stick's mob?" he asked, quietly.

Nuts nodded dismally. "I don't know why, though — it just seemed a good idea at the time. I wish I'd never run into the guy. He just pushes you around all the time. He's a psycho — I really detest the guy."

Renton took the Coke can from Nuts' hand,

pressed the ring-tab and took a swig. "It would get him off your back if I put him away for a while. I could put in a word for you."

"No, he'd probably murder me." Nuts wouldn't trust anything to keep the half-deranged Stick away.

Renton made a quick calculation, trying to weigh up the advantages. In the end he said, "I could leave you out of it entirely."

That was a different proposition, and Nuts had to consider it. If Stick was put away, Nuts could return to a normal life. His eyes peered hard at the darkness, making sure that no one was listening. "Are you serious?"

Renton shrugged. "I saved your life, didn't I?"

"Yeah, I guess you did," said Nuts thoughtfully.

"Do you want to make it a deal then?"

Nuts thought a little longer. "I might do, I'm considering it. You won't get me involved though?"

"I won't get you involved," said Renton.

That was all that Nuts needed. "Okay. Let's go get him," he said grimly.

Chapter Thirty

A little way beyond Down Street station, in a long straight stretch of tunnel, Stick caught up with the girls.

"There they are," he said, grimly. His long quest was over; he could finally see Sarah ahead of him. In his excitement at finding her he had almost forgotten what he came for – all he knew was that he wanted to pay the girl back for running rings round him. He had forgotten about the knife and the notebook; he didn't remember the wallet now. It was swept away on a great wave of viciousness.

"Right, let's get them," he murmured. "You take out the blonde one, leave the dark-haired girl to me."

This came as something of a shock to Johnny D. It was not what he wanted to hear – they had been playing a game so far, but now things were getting serious. He didn't want to start beating people up, especially a tough girl like Nikki Deveraux. She was *bigger* than him. She'd probably pulverise him.

"Erm – couldn't we wait for Nuts?" he asked miserably, giving Stick a pathetic look as he felt his heart slowly sinking down through his chest. "I thought we were only following them," he whimpered. "I thought we were just chasing them." His thin face crumpled. He didn't want to get beaten up.

Stick wasn't even listening, he was already forging on ahead. His lips were foaming, his limbs trembling with tension.

Johnny was trembling himself, but for rather different reasons. He'd never seen a man start to foam before. It was like looking at a mad dog, and he glanced over his shoulder in the hope that somebody might rescue him. "I could stay here a while and make sure nobody's following us—"

"Don't be ridiculous," said Stick. "Get yourself here with me." Grabbing hold of Johnny's shoulder, he pushed him roughly ahead of him. "You take the blonde one."

"Erm – right." Johnny bit his lip. He was utterly miserable. He was feeling a bit sick, really. It wasn't what he'd imagined – it wasn't how things were supposed to be. He wondered if he could get away with pretending to break his leg.

And he was running out of time – they were closing in fast on the unsuspecting girls. He gave a startled squeak as Nikki's dog turned to look at him. . . .

"Oh Sarah, they're here again!" said Nikki despairingly, as she looked over her shoulder. "Come on, run! Come on, Sam! Let's get out of here!"

Sam, however, seemed to have a few ideas of his own. He'd decided he'd found out where most of their problems were coming from and seemed to think that maybe it was time that he helped put a stop to them. He went sprinting down the tracks, straight at Johnny and Stick.

"*Wagh!*" Johnny gave a short scream as the ancient grey dog made right for him. He fell over backwards, with the dog clinging on to his arm. "He's got me, he's got me!" he cried, but Stick didn't turn back to help him; he was too intent on chasing after the fleeing girls.

"*Ow!* My arm! Ow, my arm!" Johnny thrashed around helplessly, trying to kick the dog, but making little impression on him. The dog had become quickly worn out by his unaccustomed exertions and had slumped across Johnny's chest.

"Get off me!" cried Johnny. "Get off me! What's the matter with you?"

The old dog gave a great, mournful sigh. He was totally shattered.

A little further back down the tracks, Renton heard the commotion. "That sounds like them," he said, breaking into a rapid trot.

"Yeah, it sounds like Johnny," said Nuts. "Look — can I just go home now?" He didn't want to get any closer to Stick than he had to. He didn't want Stick to know of his involvement, and have him haunting him for ever more. His face looked bleached as he glanced around nervously. "Can I beat it?"

"Go on," said Renton. "I'll take it from here." He didn't think Nuts would be of any use anyway.

But Nuts had already fled like a greyhound into the night. At his back, the detective looked grim as he closed in on the unsuspecting Stick. He'd waited a long time for this. He was about to put a few things straight.

Chapter Thirty-one

Johnny finally managed to roll the dog off him, just as Renton came bowling out of the darkness. "Hey, Mister – he bit me, he bit me!" he cried in a high voice.

Renton didn't have time to stop. He shoved the boy aside as he glimpsed Stick up ahead of him, about sixty metres off, gaining on the girls.

Johnny got to his feet just as Billy pelted down the track, and was pushed to the ground for a second time.

"Will you get out of the way?" muttered Billy, as he hurried on in pursuit of Stick.

As Johnny got up again, he decided it might be a good time to leave quietly. Being one of Underworld's hoodlums wasn't all it was cracked up to be – not when you were Johnny's size. It was too easy to find yourself man-handled.

"I hope you all tread in dog-dirt!" he cried, but nobody listened to him. He limped away, grumbling miserably like a sour old man.

At Hyde Park station the girls were clambering on to the platform. The place was deserted, the last train had already passed through and the station was closing down. There was no one around to help them. Nikki was having problems with her bad leg – she could hardly climb off the line and was wincing at every slight movement.

"I've had enough of this!" cried Sarah. Is he going to chase us for ever?" She turned around angrily as Stick charged out from the tunnel's depths. "I'm sick of you!" she cried. "Pick on someone your own size."

It was brave and defiant, and at the same time a little hopeless, because Stick just looked up at her and grinned. "Yeah? So what?" he said.

Sarah glared at him, panting, her eyes glittering with tension. She put her hand in her pocket and grabbed his flick-knife. "You keep away from me," she whispered. "I'm warning you, keep away from me."

"What are you going to do?" came Stick's mocking reply. "Are you going to cut my heart out?"

"I might do!" she cried. "Keep away from me!" She held the knife out towards him, then suddenly threw it angrily, so that it fell beside the track's live rail. Tossing the small notebook after it, she said, "If you want them, go and get them back. But just stop chasing around after us, will you?"

It seemed a reasonable proposition, but Stick wasn't about to buy it. This business had gone on so long now, he wanted to make the girls suffer for it. "I can't do that, because you got me mad," he said. "And when I get mad, I get angry—"

"Oh, don't be so stupid!" said Sarah. "Leave us alone, will you? We haven't done anything to you." She was growing frustrated, and her hands clenched into unaccustomed fists.

"I'm going to sort you two out," said Stick, taking a leisurely step forward. As he reached out to grab Sarah, Renton hauled himself off the line.

"It's me you want," he said, quietly. "Leave the girl alone."

There was a strange calm as Stick turned to face Renton, as if the world was holding its breath. They had waited a long time to arrive at this.

"What do you want?" murmured Renton, keeping his eyes on Stick's knuckled hands. "Do you want to call it a day, or try to make even more trouble?"

A cold grin showed on Stick's face. "You don't know what trouble is," he said, as he slipped his hand into his pocket and pulled out another knife. The blade shot out from the hilt. "I didn't come unprepared. I always knew you'd come after me – I've been waiting for it." He held the knife out ahead of him and dropped into a fighting crouch. "Come and get me," he murmured. "Come and get me, filth!"

Just then a cry rang out from behind.

"I'm coming, Sarah! Don't worry, I'm coming!"

The whole group turned in amazement as Billy came thundering out of the dark tunnel. "I'm coming to save you!" Billy leapt for the platform's edge, missed his footing and fell back. Picking himself up, he tried to repeat the exercise, but the alcohol seemed to have taken him over again.

"What's going on?" cried Stick, as Billy thrashed around below him.

"I'm gonna get you," said Billy, feebly.

Stick suddenly burst into laughter. "Hey, you're starting to frighten me!" He stopped laughing as he turned back towards Renton. And he wasn't smiling at all as he closed in on the detective. "Okay, Renton," he murmured. "It's time to finish this."

Chapter Thirty-two

Sam stood snarling like a wolf at the entrance to the tunnel, watching the two men. Ever since that thin guy had appeared they'd done nothing but charge around the place. He was getting too old for it. And he didn't like the guy, either.

He began to creep forward as Stick waved his knife under Renton's nose. It was time to sort these people out. In the distance he could hear an empty train rolling down the line on its way to the depot, racing to get home.

Billy climbed to his feet, suddenly sober. "There's a train coming!" he yelled. "There's a train coming!" He hauled himself on to the platform as the grey dog went charging by. "Look out, there's a dog coming too!" But no one heard his cry. They were too intent on the tussle taking place on the platform.

Sam launched himself at Stick, who gave a cry and went stumbling backwards, straight towards the tracks. The dog's jaws locked on his arm, and Nikki gave a cry of alarm as the pair teetered dangerously on the platform's edge. She made a wild grab for Sam as his legs slipped from under him. Still clutching Stick, he toppled backwards, and fell towards the tracks.

"Hey! One of you. Get him off!" cried Stick. "Get this dog off me!" But it was too late – he seemed to fall in slow motion, performing an ungainly cartwheel as his hands clutched dramatically at the unsympathetic air.

The man wrapped his arms round the dog as they both tried to save themselves. But it was too late. The ground rushed up to meet them and the train ploughed on regardless as they fell directly into its path in a clumsy embrace. There was a confused jumble of legs and a stifled scream from the startled Stick – then no sound at all, but a squeal from the passing train. It seemed to be clicking like a monstrous type of sewing machine as it thundered by, intent on driving stitches into every inch of the shining track.

"Stop, stop!" shouted Billy. "It's killed them! It's killed them!"

Nobody moved. Even when the train had disappeared out of sight and left a numbing silence hanging in its wake, no one dared walk to the edge and look down on the tracks.

"Did it kill them?" asked Sarah.

"I don't know," muttered Renton, as he finally forced himself to move forward and take a cautious look. He peered over reluctantly, and stood for a long time at the scene. "The dog's all right, but I can't see any sign of Stick. He must have been dragged off by the train."

"Do you think it killed him?" asked Sarah, as she managed to take a few unsteady steps herself.

"No. No, knowing Stick, he probably managed to grab hold of it," said Renton. "That's the kind of thing he would do, he's mad, crazy. He's probably been carried off down the tunnel, shrieking like a loon." He shook his head in amazement. "You've got to hand it to him, he can be pretty cool. He's some kind of survivor. He must love life in Underworld." He shook his head again. He couldn't believe what Stick had just achieved.

"What about Sam?" shouted Nikki, as she ran to look over the edge. "Sam, oh, look at him, he's scared – are you okay, Sam?"

The dog looked up from the trough where he'd flattened himself in the dirt. He wagged his tail rather feebly as Nikki sprang down off the platform to help him off the tracks.

"What about you?" said the detective, turning towards Sarah. "Are you okay?"

"Yes," she nodded. "A little scared, that's all."

Renton turned and stared down the silent track. "He's still out there. I can sense it. We haven't got him yet."

Sarah looked over his shoulder, into Underworld's unrelenting gloom. She could sense it too. Stick was still on the loose. "What are you going to do?" she asked, quietly.

Renton shrugged, and gave a weary sigh. "I don't know. Keep on going after him, try to track him down somewhere. It's kind of hard to get rid of them, hard to clean up the bad guys. . . . What about you?" he said, as Billy wove his way towards the waiting pair.

"I've got a headache," said Billy. "And I feel sick, I feel all shaken up. I want to go home now. I think I've had enough of this."

"So have I," whispered Sarah. "I want to go home too." She almost cried as she flung her arms fiercely round Billy's neck, burying her face in his shoulder.

They stood embracing for a long time, trying to wipe out their nightmares, as Nikki watched from the tracks and gave a rueful smile. After a time she put her hand on the dog's neck and ruffled his fur. "I think it's time for us to go too. I can't stand this sloppy stuff."

The girl slipped out of the station while Billy and Sarah clung on to each other. Looking back once from the entrance, she vanished down the line.

Only the detective saw her leave, and he made no move to stop her. She was from the darkness. She belonged to Underworld.